In The Beginning

It is just after midday and it is hot and stuffy. Although Thomas will not be home until after four o'clock, Carole's friends have left the house, leaving her time to clean and tidy the sitting room before Thomas and Jamie returns home.

The curtains and one window vent are open in the sitting room, allowing fresh air in to neutralise the perfume odour and keep the room cool.

Carole locks the front entrance door, removes the key as a safety measure and puts it on the mantelpiece.

Jamie will not be home until half-past-five because she is taking part in an after school activity.

The volume on the radio is slightly above normal because she likes listening to music while she works.

The cutlery and crockery from the mornings' breakfast are still on the dining table, and there is a whiff of burnt toast in the dining area but the odour is stronger in the kitchen.

The window in the kitchen is closed but the vent is open and the door from the kitchen that leads onto the patio is closed but unlocked. She switches on the washing machine and goes upstairs to vacuum.

The droning sound from the washing machine and the high-pitch whirr from the vacuum cleaner slightly drowns' the music.

Thomas arrives home before four o'clock; he unlocks and quietly opens the front entrance door, staggers into the hallway and quietly closes and locks the door. He hears the vacuum cleaner and is about to go upstairs but changes his mind. He quietly engages the top and bottom bolts on the door, removes his key and stands for a few seconds in the hallway.

Thomas opens the door from the hallway that leads into the sitting room and stands for a few seconds before calling in a loud voice, *"Carole, Carole, Carole."* There is no reply from Carole and he continues into the room.

He goes to the radio and listens to the music for a few minutes but the whirr from the vacuum cleaner and the drone from the washing machine are intolerable. He leaves the radio and goes towards the dining area, glancing at the dining table before going into the kitchen.

Whilst in the kitchen, he closes the window vent, locks the door and removes the key.

Carole is still vacuuming and is unaware that Thomas is in the house.

Thomas goes back into the dining area, picks up a cup from the table and inspects it. He picks up a knife, puts it in one of his coat pockets and mutters, *"The useless bitch, she does fuckall when I'm not here. I'll teach her a fucking lesson."*

Thomas turns up the volume on the radio, closes the window vent, and curtains in the sitting room. He leans against the mantelpiece, and complains, *"Curtains and windows open, bloody dirty cups from morning and all this fucking noise. The useless bitch."*

My
Mummy
Won't Wake Up

My Mummy Won't Wake Up

Alvis Younge

authorHOUSE®

AuthorHouse™
1663 Liberty Drive
Bloomington, IN 47403
www.authorhouse.com
Phone: 1-800-839-8640

Published by AuthorHouse   03/19/2012

ISBN: 978-1-4678-8924-7 (sc)
ISBN: 978-1-4678-8923-0 (e)

ELISABETTA 14/4/2012

The raised volume completely drowns the drone from the washing machine and the whirr from the vacuum cleaner.

Thomas shouts louder but not over the volume of the radio. *"Carole, Carole, are you bleeding deaf? Get down here now you useless bitch."* Carole does not hear Thomas and continues vacuuming.

After a few minutes, she stops vacuuming and notices the volume on the radio is louder. Fearing that she might not hear the doorbell or the telephone, Carole decides to turn down the volume and makes her way downstairs but as she reaches the bottom of the stairs she hears, *"Carole, I said get your arse down here or I'm coming up, and if I do, you won't fucking like it."*

Carole is taken aback by the unexpected command and apologises. *"Sorry Thomas, I didn't know you're home. I didn't hear you, I'm coming."* She quickly enters the room and sees Thomas is standing portentously with one hand on the back of a chair, and in the other hand the empty cup he picked up from the dining table. She stops, panics and looks around the room to see if one of her friends is in the house with Thomas. Carole composes herself and repeats, *"Sorry Thomas, I—"* Thomas is angry and interrupts. He gesticulates, *"Shut up you stupid bitch. When I call you, I expect you to fucking answer me. I called you several times. I have been standing here for nearly five bloody minutes. It stinks in here and all the fucking noise; you know I do not like noise in the house. Have you had those lay-about bitches in my house again?"*

Carole not only dares to interrupt Thomas but she also contradicts him. *"Thomas, It's not just your house, it is our house and our home. I wish you would stop using bad language, especially in the house because Jamie might hear you*

3

and start repeating what she—" Carole quickly realises she had not only interrupted Thomas but also challenged him and, having realised her error, stops talking and prepares herself for the verbal abuse she has become accustomed. The interruption, contradiction and challenge infuriate Thomas.

Carole moves towards the radio and as she is about to turn down the volume, Thomas throws the cup towards her, narrowly missing her and smashing into the wall behind the radio. She is startled and unable to move. There follows an onslaught of verbal abuse from Thomas. This is a new and unexpected departure from the daily verbal abuse she has become accustomed.

Although Carole is fearful of Thomas, she is not afraid of him. She usually dismisses his ranting and fits of temper as exasperation, brought on after his mother abandoned him, and the sudden death of his father. There are other reasons and excuses for his anger, with which Carole sympathises but she did not anticipate the departure from his verbal abuse, or the onset of such ferocity of his aggression.

Thomas continues his verbal abuse as he approaches Carole. She makes another attempt to lower the volume on the radio before speaking to Thomas. Carole thinks lowering the volume would prevent him accusing her of raising her voice but he angrily demands, *"Don't fucking touch it."* She contradicts Thomas. *"But you don't like it so loud."* Thomas replies, *"Well I do now, so leave it alone or I'll break your fucking arm."* He continues. *"What have you done all morning? The dirty cups from breakfast are still on the table and it stinks in here. It fucking stinks."*

Thomas turns away, goes back into the kitchen and checks the door is locked.

Carole is shocked and dumfounded by the sudden and unexpected change in his behaviour. She looks at the indentation in the wall and mutters, *"Oh-my-god, what's got into him? That could have been my face or head. I can't smell any alcohol only that funny smell on his breath so he's not drunk, perhaps I should ask him."* She looks at the scattered pieces from the broken cup, moves away from the radio and follows him, trembling with fear, but only reaches the dining area. Thomas comes out of the kitchen, slams the kitchen door behind him, points towards the sitting room and snarls, *"Get back in there you stupid bitch, I'm not finish with you."*

The savage tone of his voice jolts Carole; she steps back and stares at him in disbelief. His eyes are exceptionally wide and he appears to be looking straight through her, clenching his fist and slavering as he grits his teeth. Carole has not seen him looking or behaving that way before and cannot think of a reason for the sudden change in his behaviour. Thomas continues walking towards her and as he takes off his coat, the knife falls out of the pocket. As he picks up the knife, Carole cries out, *"For god's sake Thomas, what is wrong with you? Why are you being like this with me? What are you going to do with that knife? You're frightening me. Oh my god please stop it, stop it, and put it down, please."*

Carole panics, she hurries to the front door but it is locked and the key is removed; she thinks of going to the back door but Thomas is blocking her path. She realises there is no escape because the windows and doors are locked. As Thomas walks slowly and threateningly towards her, Carole momentarily reflects; *"Why did he turn up the volume on the radio despite his hatred of loud noises in the house? Why has he taken the key from the doors? Why did he close the curtains and windows? Why did he throw the cup at me?"* She feels trapped, she has no idea of his intensions and doesn't know what to prepare for but she pleads, *"Please, Thomas, talk to me, tell me. What have I done? Tell me, what is wrong? Stop it you're scaring me. Please put down the—"* Thomas barks, *"Shut-up, just shut-up or I'll smash your bleeding face in and don't fucking answer me back."*

Thomas hurls the knife into the dinning area he turns and lunges at Carole punching the side of her head. The force of the blow sends her reeling sideways and colliding against the wall. She falls onto the floor and is lying on her side unconscious.

Carole is motionless but Thomas stands over her demanding, *"Get up, get up,"* and pushes her onto her back with his foot. He steps over her and goes back to the dining area.

Carole is regaining consciousness and attempts to get up but there is nothing to hold onto for support and she rolls onto her side. She tries again but is still dazed and falls on her back. She decides it is best to remain on the floor until the dizziness wares off.

Thomas turns around, looks at Carole and repeats, *"Get up, get up, I fucking said get up"*, and walks towards her with a wry grin. He continues, *"I know why you're still down there. You'll get what's coming to you if you don't fucking get up. You bitch."* Carole is semi-conscious as Thomas straddles her and mutters, *"Right, bitch, you're asking for it so you'll get it."* He kicks her legs apart, removes her knickers and has sex with her while she is still dazed. Carole is aware that Thomas is having sex with her but is too weak and confused to resist.

After the act, he kicks her in the side and insists, *"Get up and clean yourself before Jamie gets home,"* and makes his way back to the dining area. Carole eventually gets up but finds it difficult to maintain her balance and collapses again. She struggles again and manages to get up but before going to the bathroom, she stares at him in silence.

Thomas does not speak but gesticulates with two fingers. He opens the curtains after Carole leaves the room, releases the bolts from the front door, turns down the radio volume and picks up the shattered remains of the cup.

Carole struggles to understand why Thomas raped her and why he is so aggressive but is afraid to ask in case he sees it as confrontation and attacks her again.

This heralds the escalation of domestic abuse and the continuation of a life of domestic violence against Carole.

The Beliefs

"He said he's sorry for hurting me and that he's going to change."
"It only happens when he's been drinking but he says he will stop drinking so much."
"I know he loves me because he tells me he does, and he often takes me out."
"He's not a bad person, he loves the children and he wouldn't hurt them."
"You don't know him like I do. He's a good man when he's not drinking."
"He gets' frustrated because of his upbringing but he doesn't mean it."
"He wouldn't manage if I leave him and take the children."

The onset of domestic abuse or domestic violence is not restricted to women, or to those of a certain age, ethnicity, culture, disability, social status, lifestyle, profession or religion. Many victims experience verbal abuse and subsequent violence from an early age through to adulthood, which in some instances, leads to eventual death.

The *early age* abuse against females of certain cultures might begin with the denial of certain basic life requirements, escalating to persecution, torture and culminating in death. For those females who have survived, the abuse might progress to sexual, not only by selected strangers but by relatives and or carers with the responsibility for taking care of the female. Some females might be raped or assaulted, sustaining serious jury and or disfigurement before reaching maturity in womanhood, and even as women.

From an early age, some boys are indoctrinated with the belief that they have total dominance over girls, regarding the girls as inferior and the boys as superior. Consequently, this indoctrination is given credence during social interventions and interactions. The assumption that males are superior to females is taken for granted in certain societies at different levels of social life. However, where there is objection to the perceived concept of male superiority, violence is often introduced to counter any objections.

Contrary to comments made about women who are caught up in domestic abusive situations, they do not seek out or encourage relationships with violent or abusive men. Men who are characteristically abusive or violent might not reveal this aspect of their character until the relationship is thriving, after which the woman becomes entrenched in seemingly never-ending abuse and violence. For many women, the verbal abuse and physical violence might not begin until their first pregnancy or after the first child. There are instances where the abuse begun *during* the first pregnancy.

History Makes The Future

A successful journey to a life of hope is determined by the level of responsibility imparted.

Statistics is a useful tool for measuring and providing national and international results of various forms of abuse and deaths in domestic situations.

Statistics shows that in domestic abuse situations, over two women per week are killed by their current or ex-partner, and that at least one in four women will experience domestic abuse and subsequent violence in their lifetime, and annually, between *one in ten* women do experience some form of domestic abuse.

The statistics also shows less than half of all incidents relating to domestic violence are reported to the police, however, in the United Kingdom (UK) the Police are frequently called about incidents of domestic violence. At least seven hundred and fifty thousand children witness domestic violence annually, and children living in such environment are at high and increased risk of developing behavioural problems, personality disorder and mental health problems.

According to various official reports and records, most of the children on the at risk register live in households where domestic abuse and violence occurs, and over half the number of children that are the subject of child protection have also experienced some form of domestic abuse and violence. Reports also identify children living in a refuge for victims of domestic abuse are not simply in the refuge to be with their mother, or because they have nowhere else to go, the children are also victims of domestic abuse.

The majority of domestic abuse victims are in the main women but children and men are often victims of domestic abuse and violence. However, women are considerably more likely to experience repeat and severe forms of abuse, including sexual, and girls are likely to experience the reoccurrence of abuse and violence in womanhood.

Domestic abuse might be physical (including sexual), psychological, economic deprivation, intimidation and stalking. The abuse and violence, which mainly takes place within an intimate or family-type relationship, creates a pattern of unacceptable force, threats and controlling behaviour. This level of abuse and violence can and do occur in a range of relationships including homosexual, lesbian and bisexual as well as within extended families.

Although the majority of abusers discovered are male, they are also female abusers.

Female abusers, for whatever reason, do not receive the same level of publicity or public condemnation as male abusers, seemingly, because male victims are more reluctant to report the abuse than female victims are. The reluctance of some male victims to report domestic abuse by a female could stem from sarcastic comments such as, *"He is too weak."* "She is *in charge.*" "She is *the boss.*" "She *wears the trousers"* and several other humiliating comments. The male victim might see such humiliating and degrading comments as reasons for not reporting the abuse.

The desire of the abuser to gain control over their victim might be given as a reason for their abusive or violent behaviour, although this is not always the case. Such behaviour, which might be *subtle,* might originate from a sense of *entitlement or self-professed superiority* that is often supported by sexist, racist and other discriminatory attitudes.

Even though the risk to those victims who continue to live in the abusive relationship might be high, leaving the relationship does not mean the abuse or violence will reduce or stop. The period between planning to leave and actually leaving the relationship is considered the most dangerous for victims, especially women. It is also dangerous if a child is or children are living in the relationship, particularly if there is the need to take the child or children out of the abusive environment.

The majority of children living in an abusive household will either witness the abuse and violence, or be aware of the abuse or violence, and in about half of all domestic abuse situations where they are children, sadly, the children also become victims of the abuse and subsequent violence.

Who Is Paying The Costs

As well as the financial cost to the individual and the family, domestic abuse and violence also costs society. The estimated annual cost to society in financial terms is in excess of £23 billion and rising, including the governments' contribution, which is reported to be in excess of £3 billion. They are other costs associated with domestic abuse, however, although the other costs are not hidden, there are difficult to collate.

Despite national and international publicity, domestic abuse and violence continues to be a hidden and sometimes overlooked crime. Most abusers do not think or acknowledge it is a crime to be abusive or violent against their partner or children, whilst some victims will often try to hide the crime by keeping it from family, friends, and the authorities, or by making excuses for the crime on the abusers' behalf.

Reasons for non-disclosure of the crime by some victims might range from; feeling *ashamed* or *guilty* at being the victim of abuse, expressed *love* for the abuser, *dismissing* the abuse as a *one off incident* or being *afraid* to tell anyone, fearing *more* and or *severe* abuse or violence.

For all these reasons, and many others, the victims are likely to experience several attacks before finding the courage to talk to friends or relatives, or report the abuse to the police or to other authority. On average, *thirty-five* domestic assaults happen before the assaults are reported to the proper authority.

A Loving Family

Living together is not just being together. Living together includes sharing and supporting

This is the story of *Carole Riley*, a loving and caring mother, who, from an early age witnessed domestic abuse and relentless violence against her mother *Pauline Riley* by her father *Fred Riley*. Carole subsequently became a victim of domestic abuse by her father during her teenage years. Although Fred did not kill Pauline by any physical means at that time, the abuse and violence hastened her eventual death.

As fate would have it, *Carole* also became the victim of domestic abuse and relentless violence at the hands of her husband *Thomas*, who had not witnessed domestic abuse or violence in his family, nor was a victim of domestic abuse or violence. Thomas's abusive behaviour was seemingly triggered by the onset of emotional and personality problems because of the domestic disruption in his family.

Carole did not enjoy her family's lifestyle and confessed to having a strong desire to be part of happy family gatherings, family outings and family entertainment. She frequently endured disturbed and sleepless nights listening to Pauline sobbing, crying and pleading with Fred to stop the incessant abuse and threats against Pauline. Carole longed for a good night sleep without being awaken but suffered the recurrence of terrifying nightmares of the violence.

However, the shouting and violence persisted, drastically affecting her health and education.

Adults, parents and some professionals often proclaim that children are resilient; however, not all children are as resilient as it might appear. There is also the belief that children in general are able to, and some do, cope exceptionally well with stress and traumas.

Such beliefs might be encouraged because most children are generally reluctant to express or discuss their emotions in detail with parents or even with peers. Most children are also reluctant to dwell on the affects of an incident fearing ridicule or isolation by parents or peers. Another reason a child may not be forthcoming about expressing their feelings might be their lack of ability to put into words their experiences.

When a child is hurting—emotionally or physically, silence about the reason or source is one way of coping with the pain or trauma, particularly when it appears to the child that adults—in particular parents—are not interested or listening to them.

In incidents of stress and trauma, adults generally take the view that the child will *soon get over it.* Such a view might prevent the adult from recognising the emotional or physical changes the child is displaying at that time.

Children will generally display several emotional expressions when the distress becomes unbearable such as, isolating themselves, retreating to the privacy of their personal space, segregating themselves from other family members and friends, refusing to eat—with the onset of serious health problems, becoming angrier, destructive and in the extreme, becoming suicidal.

A physical encounter is not always the cause or only reason for trauma among children. It might be caused by what the child or children have witnessed or heard for the first time or over a period. The affects on a child or some children living with domestic violence will vary but is likely to manifest itself later in adult life.

Thomason and Shirley Baker had four children—three girls and one boy. The Baker family was stable and loving, providing an environment in which the children were safe healthy and well behaved. The third child was a boy whom they named *Thomas,* had the best education the family could afford at that time; however, his education did not include attending University.

Thomason was a qualified accountant and worked at the local office of a large national company, which was within walking distance from his house. He was a typical family man—if there is such a person, easy going, and courteous, caring and hard working, and was well-known and respected in the community. Certain neighbours and friends often sought his professional assistance with accounting and tax matters.

Thomas made sure his family had the best he could afford but was mindful of what was best for the family and in particular the children. Despite being *laid-back* and easy going, there were certain things that made him angry but he avoided loosing his temper or showing his anger in front of the children.

There were *favourites* among the siblings in Thomason's family when he was growing up but he was determined not to have favourites among his children. He neither favoured, neglected nor rejected any of the children, and avoided making any of them feel they were his or Shirley's favourite. He frequently reminded Shirley that each child was an individual and as such, each child must be treated as an individual. Although Thomason was generally easy going, he was particularly strong on principals, discipline and equality but overlooked the affect his stance had on the rest of the family, especially his wife Shirley. Shirley did not always agree with him or with all of his principles but in the interest of harmony, she respected and supported him, which served as an example to the children.

Before Shirley married Thomason, she worked as a Nursing Sister at a General Hospital. After they were married, she resigned her post at the hospital because of the travelling distance from their new home, and worked as a senior practice nurse at the local Health Clinic. She was somewhat domineering and stubborn, presumably form her upbringing but because of her love and respect for Thomason, she avoided showing her dominance or stubbornness.

Shirley was the oldest of three sisters and, in keeping with tradition regarding family values and upbringing; her parents expected her to keep the other children in check, which taught her the meaning of responsibility from an early age. Her siblings respected her word and decisions, and her parents supported her actions.

Her stubbornness manifested itself whenever there was something she desired or felt it was to her advantage. She wasn't particularly ambitious but was intelligent enough to recognise a potential opening in her career. Her promotion to Nursing Sister was rapid, leaving a number of her counterparts still struggling to be considered for promotion to the next but lower level than she. Shirley created an opening for her promotion to Practice Manager at the

Health Clinic but she became pregnant before the Directors approved the position.

After the birth of their first child, Thomason decided he would be the sole breadwinner because he had a well-paid job and insisted Shirley gave up her work to take care of the child and any subsequent children.

Shirley was unhappy with his suggestion at first, and felt her independence would be hampered but after carefully considering the advantages associated with being a fulltime mother, she agreed to give up her work and be an *at home mother* to the child and children.

Thomason regularly attended finance meetings at the company's main office, which was some distance from his home and from the local office. The location of the main office meant leaving home early and often returning late evening. The demand for regular financial reports increased and after the birth of the second child, his visits to the main office became more frequent and requiring him to be away from home overnight. In addition to his frequent visits to the main office, Thomason travelled to other branches across the country staying away from home for up to three days.

Shirley soon became frustrated, lonely and bored with Thomason's long and frequent absences, and suggested she travelled with him on some of his visits. He immediately dismissed her suggestion and responded, *"It would disturb my concentration knowing you were somewhere in a strange town with two children. Besides, taking care of the children in unfamiliar surroundings would be too stressful for you."*

Despite Shirley's protestations and attempts to persuade Thomason to allow her to travel with him, he was adamant she should not accompany him but promised he would do what he could to reduce the number of meetings and the frequency of staying away over-night. Thomason also promised he would keep in touch regularly during the day as well as after each meeting. Shirley patiently listened to his promises and reluctantly accepted the compromise but it was not sufficient to satisfy her longing, and as the weeks passed, her emotional wellbeing became more affected by his long and frequent absence from home.

Shirley felt trapped because she was unable to work and with no other meaningful interest outside the home; she exercised her dominance and demanded an in-depth discussion about her present and future life. During the discussion, Thomason suggested as a further compromise, whenever he is away for more than two days, she could accompany him, or if she preferred, she could have a night out with her friends, provided there was someone suitable to take care of the children during her absence.

Shirley welcomed the suggestion to accompany him but the idea of a night out with friends was more appealing and wasted no time enquiring who might be most reliable as a baby sitter, and the going rate for baby-sitting.

Shirley enjoyed the new freedom Thomason had bestowed upon her and during that time, she reunited with some old friends, she made new friends, revisited old haunts and acquired new experiences but always made sure she returned home to be with the children before Thomason arrive. On occasions, one of her friends would stay over-night but Shirley always made sure the visit did not interfere with her domestic life or Thomason's work life.

During Shirleys' pregnancy with their third child, Thomason became his company's Chief Accountant, which brought additional benefits and responsibilities. One of the additional responsibilities entailed travelling to major national and international suppliers, which took him away from home for up to two weeks. However, neither Thomason's additional responsibilities nor his extra income was sufficient to reduce her frustration or boredom. She became increasingly depressed with the frequency and length of his absences and often made her feelings known but Thomason was adamant and tried to convince Shirley his absences were necessary because it was his job.

Shirley regularly met with her new circle of friends during her newfound freedom, which included male friends. The friendship with one particular male friend, Derrick, developed and soon became a serious affair.

Derrick lived alone after Fiona his partner of fifteen years left him for a more seemingly rewarding life in Australia with a business executive. However, she could not adapt to life down under and returned after one year. Fiona hoped that upon her return, she and Derrick would rekindle their relationship but the previous rejection was too painful and he refused to allow her back into his life.

Although Derrick lived only half hours' drive from Shirley, he did not visit her at home but met in out of town restaurants and coffee shops. Derrick did not have any children so he was particularly pleased when Shirley announced she was pregnant with her forth child, because he assumed he was the father. He hoped Shirley's pregnancy would hasten the end of her marriage to Thomason but after a few weeks, she confirmed her husband Thomason is the father. Derrick was, to say the least, somewhat disappointed and told Shirley it would be too painful to continue seeing her while she was carrying Thomason's child. The affair faded but they remained friends and continued with their clandestine meetings.

After Thomason became a Director with his company, he took control of the local branch. His promotion, in many respects, hastened the end of the secret affair between Shirley and Derrick. Thomason's promotion brought him additional financial security culminating in a very good standard of living for his family but it also brought him a new circle of friends. He regularly entertained other Directors and their families in keeping with his status but appeared to have little time for the friends he had before his promotion.

However, Shirley kept in touch with their original friends because she did not have much—if anything—in common with Thomason's new friends, and only associated with them by invitation. She felt isolated, became despondent with her new life style and in desperation got in touch with Derrick for companionship and emotional comfort.

Thomason and Shirley regularly argued and disagreed with each other but mainly on matters of principle. Although he was not of an insensitive nature, Thomason appeared to lack empathy. He appeared unable to recognise Shirley's emotional changes and needs but was never verbally, emotionally or physically abusive towards her, and always made sure the children were not present during an intense argument. As far as Thomas and his sisters were concerned, they had two loving parents who never had an intense argument, who never fell out with each other, who were never abusive towards them or each other and never used foul language or became involved with anyone in a non-marital relationship.

Sometime after the birth of her fourth child, Shirley rekindled the affair with Derrick and met in secret during the day but always made sure she arrive home before the children did. She became more adventurous and, consumed with passion, suggested meeting Derrick at his home some afternoons. He agreed but insisted she leave his home at a reasonable time so as not to arouse Thomason's suspicions, which might put an end to their meetings and affair.

The anxiety about keeping the affair from Thomason and the children was becoming unbearable. Shirley found it difficult to make eye contact with Thomason and although he did not question her about friends or friendships, she was overwhelmed with guilt and assumed he was becoming suspicious.

After months of living a double life with Derrick, Shirley was unable to contain the deception and in the end confessed her infidelity to Thomason. She also spoke of her intention to leave the marital home to live with Derrick. Thomason was devastatingly heartbroken and after weeks wrestling with his emotions and weeks of almost silence—except for questions relating to the children's welfare, promised he would forgive her because he was still very much in love with her.

As the weeks passed, Thomason did everything he could to persuade Shirley to remain in the marital home, if only for the sake of the children but her mind was made up to end the marriage.

Shirley did not discuss her decision in detail with the children but reassured them Thomason was a good father and that she would always love and be there for them. She eventually left the marital home and moved into Derrick's home. Thomas had earlier celebrated his seventeenth birthday and could not comprehend why his mother would abandon him and the rest of the family.

The separation was unbearable and Thomas soon became depressed.

After Shirley's confession of her infidelity, Thomason was neither violent or vindictive towards her while she was still in the marital home, nor verbally abusive during the separation. He made several unsuccessful attempts to reunite with Shirley but her love for Derrick was stronger than his persuasions and she ultimately rejected him.

During the separation, Thomasons' health began failing and gradually deteriorated. He lost his position as a Director and eventually his job, which made him severely depressed.

The rejection, stress and depression took its' toll on Thomason's health and he died two years later. A few months after Thomason's death, Derrick and Shirley moved to a different part of the country.

Thomas did not connect with Derrick because he assumed it was Derrick alone who broke up the relationship but kept in touch with Shirley because he still loved her, however, he lost contact with Shirley after she moved away from the area. He spoke to several of her former friends as well as family members whom he assumed would know her whereabouts but to no avail. Some of Shirley's family had rejected her and several of her friends distanced themselves form her, which reduced Thomas's chances of finding her. Thomas became angry with Shirley, blamed her for the subsequent demise of the family, and sought to quell his anger, frustration and depression by chain smoking, using illegal drugs on a small scale and drinking excessively.

Thomas's personality changed dramatically during his search for and anger with Shirley. He was no longer tolerant, patient, understanding or someone with whom one could reason, with bouts of overwhelming sadness, anger, and negativity, hatred—mainly of women, frustration and boredom. He developed patterns of unstable and sometimes turbulent emotions and his behaviour was reminiscent of a child rejected or abandoned early in its life. Although the disruption in the family occurred in his early life, the full impact of the disruption did not occur until much later in his life. Throughout most of those traumatic times, Thomas remained in the family home.

Personality Disorder

A person is not always judged by how successful they are, but by how they respond to a challenge and disagreement.

Personality Disorder is a condition that is not as widely publicised, recognised or investigated as other psychological and psychiatric conditions. The cause of Personality Disorder is not fully known but it is assumed that genetic, family and social factors play a role in its onset. Sufferers with the condition have long-term patterns of unstable and or turbulent emotions, such as negative feelings about others—particularly those closes to them, and about themselves. These inner experiences often cause the sufferer to take impulsive actions and have chaotic relationships.

Studies suggest that individuals with the condition frequently experience strong and long-lasting periods of tension, precipitated by the thought of rejection, perceived failure or a feeling of being alone, despite reassurances from family and friends that they are not alone. Individuals might experience fluctuating emotions between anger and anxiety, or between depression, anxiety, and temperamental sensitivity to emotional stimulations.

There is also the tendency for sufferers to experience extreme emotional and negative feelings, which might be described as destructive or self-destructive. An individual with the condition can be particularly sensitive to the way others treat them, and might react strongly to perceived criticism or hurtfulness, even if the criticism is constructive, requested or encouraged. Other negative experiences include feelings of fragmentation, lack of identity and a feeling of being victimised despite being chosen to contribute to an activity or event.

Affection and general feelings about friends or partners often change from positive to negative within a very short time, and usually after a disappointment or perceived threat of losing a lover, partner, close family member or a good friend. Self-image can also change rapidly from extremely positive to extremely negative, triggering suicidal thoughts. Impulsive behaviour is also common, including alcohol or drug abuse, sexual recklessness, gambling and the tendency to experience recurring unbearable and overwhelming feelings of various emotions, which might include sadness, anger, anxiety, depression, hatred without just cause, emptiness, frustration, helplessness, procrastination, loneliness and boredom.

There was a period in Thomas's early life when he was in and out of relationships. He would passionately fall in love but quickly loose interest and end the relationship. Thomas made frantic efforts to ensure his lovers did not abandon or reject him even though it was he who ended the relationships.

However, to overcome his imagination of rejection and abandonment, Thomas would later rekindle the relationship but after a few months or so, he would loose interest again and end the relationship. Such was his paranoia, he often accused his friends and lovers of rejecting him despite being reassured he was included in their plans.

The relationship between Thomas and his father was one of utmost respect. He not only looked up to Thomason as a father but as an advisor and life-long supporter. Thomas identified himself with his father and tried to emulate him by discarding aspects of his own personally as well as some personal interests. Thomas was neither characteristically for nor against conformity or uniformity but saw the need to embrace them because it was what his father stood for.

Most of the young people and friends Thomas grew up with had left the district, and the few friends that remained gradually drifted away from him. People acknowledged him but only as a matter of courtesy. Thomas was slowly becoming isolated but found comfort through drinking, smoking and using illegal drugs.

The decline in his personality and rapid emotional changes prompted a friend to suggest he approach his doctor for advice about how to control his behaviour and reduce his excessive use of drugs and alcohol but the suggestion brought an angry and venomous like response from Thomas. He flatly refused to embrace his friends' suggestion and retorted, *"Look, I don't need anyone interfering in my private life. I am in control of my life and could easily give up drugs and alcohol, so you can all fuck off."* Thomas vigorously defended his god-given-right to live his life as he wishes.

Moving On

If mending the fence doesn't solve the problem, build a bridge.

Thomas' behaviour became so intolerable whilst at home, the rest of the family suggested he leave as soon as possible to avoid any violence, which he reluctantly did and left with a few belongings. He spent several months in and out of hostels, lodgings and spending the odd night with friends before he found a dingy apartment, which was about seven miles from his original home address. A couple of weeks after moving into the apartment, he met and, as usual, quickly and passionately fell in love with a woman name *Theresa*. Theresa was much older than Thomas was but the age difference was not a matter for concern, because they both had something in common—drinking alcohol, smoking and using illegal drugs. Theresa did not fall in love with Thomas, she saw him as a chance to increase her takings without any emotional attachment.

Theresa was intelligent, financially self sufficient and lived with relatives in a four-bedroom detached house, which was located in a much sought after area. Her adopted lifestyle did not reflect her status or surroundings. Theresa used as well as sold illegal drugs but tactfully, she did not sell the drugs in her area.

A few months after meeting Thomas, she suggested it would benefit both of them if they lived together in her house. As far as Theresa was concerned, the suggestion was not for romantic reasons but strictly for business.

Theresa's family knew very little about Thomas, and was apprehensive about them living together but partially accepted her decision in the hope that he might be a good influence. The family hoped he would help Theresa reduce and eventually stop her dependency on alcohol and illegal drugs.

Theresa had a higher standard of education than Thomas did; she was much more intelligent and could be manipulative. Allowing Thomas to live with her gave Theresa the opportunity to expand her racket by using him as a courier for delivering her illegal drugs, thus increasing the number of her *clients.*

As the association between Thomas and Theresa became stronger, it developed into a *partnership in crime* but without equal share of the ill-gotten gains. Thomas *progressed* from using the drugs to delivering them on Theresa's behalf, but mainly when and where it was difficult for her to make the delivery in person. Relatively easy access to drugs and enough money to buy alcohol whenever he had the urge to indulge encouraged his dependency on drugs and alcohol, which ultimately spiralled out of control.

Most of the deliveries Theresa assigned to Thomas were in areas considered dangerous but delivering the drugs made him somewhat ambitious and greedy. Thomas became greedy, which fuelled his ambition to become a dealer but both led to him encroaching on other dealers' patch.

Thomas had bouts of fearlessness and lost most of his inhibitions, especially after drinking alcohol. He became sarcastic, insulting, and careless about where he went, what he did or whom he offended.

Theresa asked Thomas to make a delivery in a park during one of her busy periods, and insisted he did not make the delivery after mid-day, because the *client* lived in one of her rival's area but he ignored her and made the delivery in the afternoon. During the delivery, the rival dealer saw him and confronted him. There was an altercation; Thomas attacked the dealer first knocking her unconscious. The dealer later complained to the Police and Thomas was arrested. During the interview, Thomas told the Police he was delivering drugs for Theresa, and that he had no idea who her supplier was. However, the Police arrested Theresa for another incident before questioning her about her drug dealing activity.

Thomas was subsequently charged with the assault and sentenced to three months imprisonment.

The incident involving Thomas and the rival dealer, and the subsequent custodial sentence frightened Theresa, prompting her to reduce her drug dealing activity but she continued using illegal drugs.

Thomas associated with several gangs during his incarceration, and within a short time became involved in illegal drug dealing among other inmates. He became familiar with other dealers outside prison as his drug dealing experience increased, but realised his sentence could be increased or his early release cancelled if he was caught, and decided to breakaway from the gangs.

Breaking away from the gangs was not easy; in fact, several gang members threatened to *slap* him whilst he was inside, and have him *attended to* when he was outside on the grounds of disloyalty and desertion. Despite pressure from the gangs, he refused to continue his involvement and during the remainder of his sentence, he managed to avoid cooperating when confronted or when threatened.

Thomas returned to live with Theresa after his release from prison, but the relationship deteriorated. He quickly lost interest after suspecting she and her family were plotting against him in a bid to prevent them forming a meaningful relationship and force him out of the house. He became aggressive, insulting and frequently made sarcastic comments about Theresa and her family.

Theresa's close friends—the ones that did not drink heavily or used illegal drugs, and several of her relatives blamed him for encouraging her to increase her drug use and illegal dealing, which wasn't the case, because Theresa used and sold drugs long before she met Thomas. Thomas blamed Theresa for using him to deliver the drugs, which lead to his eventual arrest and incarceration.

The arguments between them increased, becoming more intense with each argument. He became extremely angry, verbally abusive and threatened her with physical abuse if she did not agree to a *partnership* in her drug-dealing racket. However, Theresa was adamant she would not agree to have him as a drug dealing partner but he could not accept her decision and begun physically abusing her.

The abuse started with pushing and slapping but it soon progressed into punching and kicking. The friendship between him and Theresa's family was also rapidly deteriorating. He was disrespectful, threatening and reacted violently after assuming they were isolating him. Certain members of Theresa's family were quite outspoken and expressed their disgust with the living arrangement between him and Theresa, and Theresa warned him if he continues to be abusive—verbally or physically, he would have to leave the house.

Theresa's family grew more intolerant with Thomas's despicable behaviour, and equally impatient with Theresa for tolerating his behaviour. Theresa's older sister suggested on several occasions, that Thomas be kicked out of the house but Theresa ignored the suggestion because it was to her advantage to have him around as her courier. Thomas became furious with Theresa during one of their arguments, accused her of undermining his contribution to her profitable dealings and threatened to be-head her if she did not hand over more of the profits from her drug racket. Theresa was quite forceful with her reply. *"Look Thomas, you and I will never be partners. You will get your fixes and some pocket money and that is all, so stop pestering. If you don't like it, fuck off."*

Needless to say, her reply infuriated him. He was so angry he was unable to speak for about fifteen minutes but when he did, it was a warning to her. *"You bitch, you'll pay for this. I put my arse on the line for you. You will pay for this."*

One evening whilst they were out drinking together, Thomas said to Theresa, *"Come on, let's go for a walk and talk about money."* *"What money?"* Theresa asked. *"Look,"* Thomas snapped, *"I've been putting my arse on the line for you, dodging the other dealers night and day. I even got fucking banged for you and—"* Theresa interrupted; *"No, you were not banged up for me. It was your fucking stupid fault that got you banged up. I told you what you must not do and you did the opposite. I could have been arrested and locked up because you did not listen. Why should I give you any more fucking money?"* Thomas responded; *"You didn't have so many smack-heads before you met me and you haven't been delivering as often as I have. You owe me. You fucking owe me and I want what you owe me now."*

Theresa listened to his reasons for wanting more money as they walked side by side but she was still adamant Thomas would neither receive more money nor be a partner. Her determination to keep him out her racket incensed him; he lost control and responded as he does, and punched her in the face almost breaking her nose. Theresa stumbled backward from the force of the blow, fell onto the pavement dislocating her left shoulder and hitting the back of her head. Thomas panicked after Theresa appeared to loose consciousness but instead of calling for an Ambulance, he picked her up—semi-conscious, draped her right arm around his shoulder, as if it was a scarf, almost dragging her, took her back to the house, and stayed with her until she fully regained consciousness.

Thomas realised he could be locked up again and for much longer if Theresa or her family took legal action against him, so, as she was regaining full consciousness, he attempted to convince her that she tripped and fell backwards while she was drunk. Theresa was not convinced about the cause of her injury and asked, *"If I only fell backwards, why is my face swollen and my nose out of shape? Why didn't you call for an Ambulance? I should be in hospital. How much blood did I loose?"*

Thomas gave her several explanations but could not find one convincing enough to satisfy her. After nearly an hour trying to recollect what happened, Theresa finally remembered but did not challenge him fearing that he might become angry and violent again.

The family was horrified although not surprised, after seeing Theresa's bruises but before they had time to ask how, why, where or when she exclaimed, *"The bruises and injury happened when I fell after Thomas and I were out drinking. Don't worry, I'll be alright.*" None of the family believed her explanation and encouraged her to report the injury to the police as a vicious assault and go to A&E but Theresa refused, because involving the Police would expose her to an unwelcome investigation, which might force her to reveal her drug-dealing racket and land her in prison.

As the weeks passed, Theresa regained her strength sufficient to resume her drug-dealing racket without involving Thomas. Some bruises were still visible but not sufficient to make people stare at her. This increased his suspicion that Theresa was isolating him and confronted her. *"Hey, you fucking bitch, are you trying to cut me out? Are you trying to make me look stupid? You owe me; you fucking owe me. Fucking give me what you owe me or——"* but instead of responding with an explanation, Theresa replied, *"Hey, you fucking bastard, collect your stuff and all the other crap that belong to you and get to fuck out of my house, now. Do not contact me or come near this house again. Hurry up and get your arse out of my sight and out of my house or it won't be the Police this time, it will be the Ambulance."* Thomas felt an overwhelming sense of rejection and immediately erupted into one of his rages for about fifteen minutes. He created mayhem turning over the settee, the dining table, chairs, the bed; he emptied the cutlery draws and saturated the kitchen floor. He created more mess than damage but he paid for the damage and left.

Thomas subsequently moved to another town but could not find affordable single accommodation; however, he eventually found an apartment, which he shared with like-minded people.

This Is My Profession

There are those who take care but don't care, and there are those who care but don't take care, and there are those who just don't care.

Saundra was a well-known local prostitute whom the Police arrested several times for drunkenness and drug possession. Thomas met Saundra while she was working and soon became good friends. He was not her pimp but the friendship developed into a kind of protective relationship. *A* few months after meeting, he suggested they live together and she agreed to.

The union appeared to be gaining in strength but Thomas became jealous and disapproved of her work as a prostitute. He didn't object to her using drugs or drinking, because that was something they both had in common but he could not cope with the idea that she was having sex with other men who were mostly strangers.

Thomas took it upon himself to *look after* Saundra because he assumed she needed looking after, given the work she did and the money she was making. Saundra previously attended personal protection classes before working as a prostitute, and did not see the need to tell him, so he wasn't aware that Saundra knew how to look after herself.

The knowledge and experience in self-defence subsequently helped her to remain reasonably safe after becoming a prostitute. However, his expression of care and concern did not last very long.

Thomas frequently argued with Saundra on matters of health and safety, reminding her of the danger of unsafe sex, sex with multiple partners and the need for regular health checks. Saundra told him she appreciated his concern but was becoming fed-up with his controlling attitude and asked, *"Why are you so concerned about my sexual health?"* Thomas replied, *"Well, you should get your self checked out. I don't want to catch anything."* Saundra responded, *"Well, It's a bit late for that. You were so desperate when we first met, you were not interested in safe sex, and you just wanted to get on with it. Don't forget, it was I who insisted you wore protection the first time, and that was because I didn't want to be pregnant. Perhaps I should make sure I don't catch anything from you."*

Thomas assumed he was more experienced in personal protection and self-defence than she was, and tried several times to convince her she should trust him to take care of the money she receives from her work. Saundra asks, *"Where would you keep the money if I gave it to you, in a piggy bank, under the carpet, under the mattress or in your back pocket? It's my money and I'll take care of it, as I have always done."*

During one of their many arguments, Saundra angrily reminded him it was she who provided most of the money that paid for his drink and drugs and suggested, *"Look, if you're pissed off with me or the work I do, you should collect your stuff and get out. I do not want a pimp. You don't complain about the money so why complain about the work. I know where I can find a pimp If I want one."* Thomas wasn't used to such confrontation, especially so early in a relationship, and responded by slapping her across the face.

Despite the danger associated with her work as a prostitute, Saundra was never physically abused, even when she was drinking or under the influence of illegal drugs, so, being physically abused during an argument, particularly with her partner, was a new and unwelcome experience, one she was determined would not be repeated.

The assault brought an angry response and retaliation from Saundra. *"How dear you hit me you little bastard. No one has ever done that to me, not even one of those cantankerous bastards. I'll teach you a bloody lesson."* First, she kicked him in the groin, dropkicked him to the side of his face, which sent him sprawling onto the floor. She picked him up, held him in a headlock and promised him; *"I'll break your fucking arm or your neck if you ever do that again."* Saundra's retaliation shocked Thomas but instead of apologising for his action, he muttered his annoyance vowing, *"I'll get you for this. I'll fucking get you for this."*

Saundra gave up prostitution after becoming pregnant, because she wanted to a different life for the baby with Thomas. Thomas was please she had given up prostitution but not very please he was about to become a father. His main concern at that time was about money and asks, *"Where will the fucking money come from now? I need money to, well, we both the money."* The arguments between them continued, mostly about money but after the chastising Saundra gave him after he slapped her, he controlled his physical response.

Thomas wanted more money so that he could buy a sufficient quantity of drugs to begin dealing in earnest but Saundra refused and in his moment of frustration snapped, *"What have you done with all the fucking money you made from selling your body? You sell your body, which is easy and I sell drugs, which is fucking hard. I don't want all your fucking money, just enough to—"* Saundra interrupted; *"Look Thomas, I worked as a prostitute before I got involved with you. It's not as easy as you think it is. It is my money and I am keeping it, besides, if you want to make more money and make it quickly, you should try selling your body. Although, I don't think anyone in their right mind would want to buy your body, so maybe you should stick to buying and selling the drugs instead but without my money."*

Saundra's comments infuriate Thomas, especially the one about his body but, mindful of her condition, he contained his anger. During the following weeks, his client base increased and demand also increased, however he was unable to meet the demands and in desperation asked Saundra for a loan but she reminded him; *"I am expecting a baby and will need my money. I lost some of my income when I gave up working, so you should give up drug dealing, stop being so fucking greedy and get a job."* The remark incensed Thomas. He leapt from the chair and screamed at Saundra, *"No, no fucking no. I am not giving that up. Why not let me have the fucking money? I'll pay you back double. I thought we were mates. You bitch."*

Saundra laughs as she responds. *"You will pay me back double? You cannot even afford to pay for your booze. How long will it take you to pay me back if I agree to lend you some money?"* Thomas gritted his teeth and retorted, *"Don't you fucking laugh at me,"* and struck her against the side of her head with his clenched fist. As she stumbled, more from shock, he kicked her onto the floor, stood over her and reminded her of his promise. *"I said I'll fucking get you, pregnant or not. Don't you ever laugh at me. You bitch."*

Saundra was too dazed to retaliate but also fared retaliating might put her baby at risk of harm. Unfortunately, the fight caused Saundra to miss-carry. She was not prepared to put up with his violence and unreasonable behaviour, and quickly ended the relationship but did not return to prostitution.

After Saundra kicked him out, Thomas presupposed he was not very good at keeping relationships and decided he would remain un-attached for the time being. His main concern was having enough money to buy alcohol and a good quantity of illegal drugs—sufficient to continue his illegal drug dealing scam.

The Good Samaritan

**Love thy neighbour as yourself but if you do not love
yourself God help your neighbour.**

The morning after Saundra kicked him out, Thomas
wandered from street to street and visited the local parks
hoping to find a like-minded victim but to no avail. He
decided it would be best if he looked for work—so to speak,
in another area and headed for the next town. After several
exhausting hours looking around the town, he sat on an
upturn metal bin at the side of a Hairdresser's salon with his
head in his hands, and feeling sorry for himself.

As he pondered his next move and wondered where
he might get his next fix, a woman walking her dog and
carrying a document case, stopped, looked at him and
remarked, *"Young man, you look as if you've lost a pound and
found a penny."* Thomas is not in the mood for answering
questions or holding conversations, so he looks up at her
and looks away without speaking. The woman continues,
*"What are you looking for? Have you lost something?" Has
something happened to you?"* He looks her up and down,
looks at the dog, looks at her again and replies, *"No, nothing
has happened to me, I'm not looking for anything, and I haven't*

lost anything. I haven't found a penny but I could do with a pound. Who the fu—, who are you?"

Thomas is feeling depressed, vulnerable and alone. He is not on his best behaviour at that time and is swift with his sarcasm and rude outbursts. Being kicked out by Saundra is very fresh in his mind, and the effect of his last fix is wearing off. What little money he has is fast running out but he has no intension of stealing, begging or borrowing—least of all from a stranger. The woman continues. *"I'm Joan, some of my friends call me Sister Jo and others call me Jo. What is your name? Your bum must be cold sitting on that bin?"*

Joan was in the teaching profession for over forty years but retired early after an incident with a pupil. She is of the old school where discipline is foremost, and is intolerant with anyone who flaunts the rules. After retiring from teaching, she worked for several charities but settled for a charity that helped the homeless and destitute. Joan spent several months in East Africa as an independent support worker, where she was emotionally overwhelmed by the plight of those who were suffering—in her opinion, needlessly, because of the hypocrisy of some government officials and agencies.

As an independent support worker in a foreign country, Joan was responsible for providing her own financial support, which was becoming difficult to sustain for the full eighteen-month stint. Whilst she was in Africa, Joan approached several agencies for financial assistance but was refused. She felt the reason for the refusal was her outspokenness against their policy and approach to the suffering at that time. She once demonstrated her frustration during a meeting with an outburst. *"This is daylight robbery and corruption at the highest level. You are suppose to be helping these people but you drive around in your air conditioned cars and return to your large air conditioned houses where you pay your servants peanuts to wait on you. You should all be ashamed. You should all be locked up."*

Joan returned home heartbroken because she was unable to continue her mission due to a lack of funding. She realised there were other ways her experience and caring skills could be used, and became an active member of an evangelical church in the community.

Thomas sits up straight and then stands up. He notices Joan is wearing flat shoes but she is still taller than he is. *"What do you want from me? I just want a little peace and quiet."* Joan replies, *"You look like a lost soul that needs to be rescued and cared for. I might be able to help you."* Her comment infuriates him. *"Look you, whoever you are, I'm not lost and don't need rescuing, not even by you, besides, there's fuckall wrong with my soul."* Joan immediately and harshly rebukes him for using foul language and suggests to him, *"You should wash your foul mouth with holy water."*

He acknowledges he was disrespectful and without challenging or confronting her he accepts the rebuke by remaining silent. Thomas rarely apologises for his behaviour or hurtful actions, so, is Thomas undergoing an emotional or psychological change? Has he met his match? Is this a vulnerable young man succumbing to word power, or, is it the mind-set of a desperate or suspicious young man?

Joan mutters, *"I think it is time to help this young man control his anger and sweeten his language."* She slowly reaches into her document case, takes out a book and opens it at the marked page but before she says anything, Thomas steps back and positions himself to run away. The sight of the book makes him apprehensive, he panics, raises his hands as if in surrender and exclaims, *"Bloody hell, are you from Probation?"* Joan is regularly mistaken for belonging to various professions but never as a Probation Officer. She recognises Thomas is panicking at the sight of the book and quickly seeks to quell his fear with, *"No, no, I'm not from the Probation office and look, this book is my Bible. I always carry it with me. Would you like me to read something from this passage to you?"*

Thomas breathes a sigh of relief after Joan explains that the book is her Bible but he is still worried because he has no idea who she is, what she does or what she wants. He usually assumes command when talking to a female but on this occasion, is somewhat intimidated by Joan's pugnacious approach and feels the need to assert his dominance over Joan before she take control.

He paces backwards and forwards with both hands in his pockets, spitting on the ground several times and pretending to cough. He makes a pretend kick at the dog, leans against the Hairdressers' salon, looks directly at Joan and whilst gesticulating asks, *"Who the fuck are you? What is it you do? What do you want? First, you pretend to be a do-gooder, then you scare the shit out me with that book, which you say is a Bible, and now you want to read to me. Are you mad or just taking the piss? I don't want any of that bible and god stuff so just fuck off and leave me alone."*

Joan is no stranger to foul language. It is the language used by many in the groups she work with, however, she is unaccustomed to hearing such foul language directed at her and, although a little shocked at the verbal onslaught, she is in no mood to tolerate it from Thomas. Joan looks at him through slit eyes and with her lips pouted, she slowly puts the Bible back into the document case and responds with an incisive rebuke. *"Now listen to me you ungrateful young man, how dear you raise your foot to my dog, and speak to me like that? Watch—your—language. There is no need to speak to me like that, especially when I am being pleasant with you and trying to help you. I work with people who have very little but are grateful for what they receive and show appreciation for it. The world does not owe you anything. You should be thankful that I am a Christian. Would you talk to a man like that?"* Thomas does not tolerate dissent, especially from females but the stern talking from Joan makes him feel humble. He immediately apologises for his outburst, *"OK, you're right, sorry, I'm not having a—"* He feels he is loosing control again, stops the apology and in a calmer voice asks, *"Who are you, what do you do?"*

Joan senses Thomas is now under her control—so to speak, and is ready to listen to her words of wisdom but she does not realise it might take more than a few biblical quotations to control Thomas. Joan pulls the dog closer; she commands it to sit and beckons Thomas to do the same on the upturn bin, which he does without question. She removes the Bible from the document case and places it in the palm of her left hand. Joan assumes the preaching position and opens it at the selected chapter. Thomas looks at her inquisitively and mutters, *"Bloody-ell, she must be one of those Bible bashers."* Joan reads his lips and responds, *"No, I'm not a Bible basher but today I will deliver the words to you. You have a foul mouth but I am sure you must have a good heart. Before I begin, what is your name?"* He is puzzled by the question and asks, *"Why do you want to know my name?"* Joan replies, *"You know my name. Are you hiding from someone or the Police?"* Thomas quickly replies, *"No, I'm not. Why should I hide from the Police?"* Joan responds, *"You might have done something or is carrying something you should not, so what is your name?"* Thomas realises she is not giving up and condescendingly replies, *"OK, if you must know, it's Thomas but I don't tell every body so don't you spread* it around." "*Thank you Thomas. I think we will get along fine. Perhaps you are not as obnoxious and vulgar as you want me to believe.*"

It is many years since Thomas attended church as a Sunday school boy and had not read the Bible since that time. His absence from church meant he had long forgotten the language used by church people and mockingly replies, "*I don't know the words in that Bible book but I know what the words are on the street. The first word I want to hear begins with C, which is coke, short for Cocaine, the next word begins with M, which is money, and I need some now. There is another word that begins with S, which is supply but I'm not too bothered about that right now, I need the money first.*"

Joan ignores his sarcasm and begins, "*The reading this morning is from John chapter 3 verse 16. For God so loved the world that he gave his only begotten son, that whosoever believes in him should not perish but have everlasting life. In John chapter 15 verses 12, the Lord says, this is my commandment that you love one another as I have loved you. The Lord also said . . . .*" but before Joan had time to tell him what the Lord said, Thomas gets up, kicks the bin behind him and interrupts. "*Look, look, look, all I want right now is somewhere to sleep, enough for a pint and something to make me feel good. Can you say the word and give me any of these things?*" Joan looks at Thomas in silence as he paces back and forth. He continues, "*I'm desperate for a job and somewhere to live. Do you know where I can get a job? Can you put me up for a few nights? I'll be a good lodger. You won't hear a sound from me, unless you start that preaching stuff.*"

Joan thinks his response is her opportunity to save his soul. "*I can't find you a job, that's up to you. I suppose you—, I can let you sleep in my guest room for a few weeks but you will have to obey my house rules.*" Thomas is astounded by

Joan's offer of a bed, not just for one night but also for a few weeks. However, he is somewhat apprehensive about the house rules and wonders if the rules include allowing her to follow him to the bathroom, check what he is drinking or search his pockets for drugs. *"Ok, Ok do-gooder, what are these rules?"* Joan reminds him, *"Thomas, I told you my name is Joan but if you prefer, you can call me Jo. I promise not to call you Tom Tit."*

And so, Joan begins. *"I will expect you to say your prayers before going to bed, or we can say them together. We will say grace before the meals we have together. We can go to my church when it is family Sunday. I will read a passage to you from the Bible after our supper. There will be no smoking or drinking in my home but occasionally we might have only one glass of wine with our evening meal. There are to be no strange women, unless they are good friends, and no hanky-panky. I will not tolerate illegal drugs or addicts in my home. Always close the bathroom door when you go in. Do not leave the toilet seat up, pull the chain after and clean up your drips. I will expect a contribution to the household expenses. I'll tell you the others after you move in—if you move in."*

Thomas neither objects to nor challenges Joan's house rules at that time because he is desperate for somewhere to sleep but comments; *"Going to church and saying prayers before meals or going to bed is for Bible bashers. As for hanky-panky, I could do without that, at least for the time being but I couldn't manage without a drink or my fix. Your idea of family life is not my idea of family life; it sounds like a prison run by a do-gooder."* Joan responds, *"Well, you can take it leave it. It's my final offer."* Thomas accepts. *"Ok, OK when can I move in? If I don't like the other rules can I talk to you about them?."* *"Yes"* Joan replies, *"but it might not make any difference."*

47

Although there is no formal agreement between them, Joan assumes Thomas has accepted her terms and is ready to move into her home. She puts away her Bible whilst Thomas gathers his belongings; she gives the dog a few biscuits and together heads for her home.

Joan lived a short distance from the Salon but in the opposite direction to where he was originally heading. The living and sleeping arrangement is completed, Thomas settles into his new routine but is uneasy that Joan might be slowly converting him and wonders how he can rebel against the rules and against her way of life.

Thomas felt comfortable in his new home and decided not to challenge the house rules or question Joan's way of life. However, Joan thought nothing of bursting into song at anytime during the day or night, or delivering a short sermon after dinner on the evils of drugs, drink, sex and prostitution.

One morning after breakfast, Joan began singing, *"Shall we gather at the river, the beautiful the beautiful river."* That rendition prompted Thomas to reply; *"Ok; I'll go with you but only if I can have a proper drink when I get there."* Joan is not impressed. She suggests the remark is insulting and accuses him of being disrespectful to the meaning of the river of life.

As the weeks passed, Joan developed a fondness for Thomas but was cautious about revealing her feelings in words. She had a philosophy; *"If you're going to be a good person when you're away from home, make sure you're good when at home."* Joan catered for his domestic and culinary needs; however, she thought the way to his heart was via the *good book.*

Joan's weekend normally started on Saturdays, which she usually reserved for domestic chores and shopping. She also prepared her presentation for Sunday mornings' church service. Visitors were only encouraged if they were desperate, otherwise the weekend was strictly hers. Thomas's weekend was Friday to Monday afternoon, which was always busier than Joan's. He used his weekend to forage, whereas she uses hers to relax. Joan was not too concerned about Thomas's coming and going at the weekend or his Monday lie-in because he respected her home and her privacy.

It is Saturday night, Joan has finished her chores and is preparing for bed.

Thomas is in the nearby town attempting to sell drugs but he is disappointed because his rivals have out-smarted him and his regulars have let him down. He is also looking to satisfy his sexual needs but is short of money and is desperate to make a sale.

Joan secures the windows and doors before going to the bathroom.

Thomas is frustrated after a night without a sale and no sex but he is sober and decides he will have an earlier night, and makes his way home.

Joan finishes her ablutions and goes to bed. She reads a chapter form her Bible and falls asleep before turning off the bedside light.

Thomas arrives home and sees the light on in Joan's bedroom and the room door partly open, and calls; *"Joan, are you alright? Joan. Joan."* There is no reply from Joan. He calls again; *"Joan, are you in there?"* and goes upstairs to Joan's bedroom. He looks through the narrow opening between the door and the door frame, sees her lying on top of the bed and calls again, *"Joan, Joan are you asleep?"* but there is no reply. He stands outside the bedroom, quietly pushes the door, steps inside the room, peers around the door, goes to the bed and takes a good look at her.

Joan is wearing a short nightdress, which is revealing the top of he left thigh. Her hands are in the submission position, the Bible is next to her head on the left side and she appears to be snoring.

Thomas moves to the bottom of the bed, sees Joan is wearing only a short nightdress. The position of the nightdress reveals some of her pubic hairs. He looks at Joan, stares at the exposed section of pubic hair and quietly calls, *"Joan, Joan wake up."* He gently shakes her left foot but she is still asleep. He calls a little louder, *"Joan, wake up and get into bed you're getting cold,"* but she does not respond. Thomas leans closer to Joan's face to check she is breathing, leaves the room and partly closes the door.

Thomas goes to the bathroom; he takes a shower and changes into his pyjamas. He goes back downstairs and checks the windows and doors are secure before going back to Joan's room. The light is still on; she appears to be asleep and is in the same position.

He calls again whilst shaking her foot, *"Joan, Joan,"* but Joan is in a deep sleep.

Thomas straddles her body, picks up the Bible and places it on the side dresser. Her nightdress moves up slightly exposing more of her pubic hears.

Thomas catches a whiff of her night perfume and remakes, *"That shit smells nicer than my shit but I bet it tastes like shit. I'll stick with my shit; at least it makes me feel good."* He positions her body in the centre of the bed, places her head on a pillow, covers her with the duvet, he turns out the light, closes the door and goes back to his room.

Joan opens her eyes as she hears Thomas closing his bedroom door and sighs, *"Oh dear, I thought he fancied me. There is a glimmer of warmth and thoughtfulness beneath that troubled and rugged exterior, as well as the desire to lead a different life."*

Joan felt Thomas was struggling with his desire to be the person he once was and stop being the person he has become. There were occasions when Thomas revealed some of his desires and fears to Joan but on each occasion he would cut short the discussion for fear of revealing too much of his background and family life. Joan believed Thomas was the challenge she waited for since embracing the teachings and guidance of the Bible and since returning form West Africa. She also felt the time was right to reveal her inner desires to Thomas; however, there were other questions she needed to ask of herself.

One evening after dinner, Joan arranges the furniture in the sitting room to make it cosy for the revelation of her desires. She places a half bottle of wine and a bowl of salted peanuts on an occasional table, lights a few scented candles, turns off the overhead light, tunes in the radio to a classical music station, turns down the volume until it is just audible, summons Thomas and beckons him to sit next to her. Thomas obliges and sits next to her but not so close as to touch her. Joan gesticulates; *"Thomas, please, open and pour the wine. Have some nuts."* Thomas opens the wine, pours some into each glass and hands one to Joan. Joan takes hers, clinks glasses and together recites the alcohol anthem *"Cheers, good health cheers."*

After a few sips of wine, Joan begins extolling the virtues of Thomas, complementing him for being a caring lodger and talks about how she is looking forward to a long and lasting companionship. Thomas in turn thanks her for allowing him to stay for such a long time and compliments her cooking. After the shared shower of compliments, Joan places her half-empty wine glass on the table, gets up, turned off the radio, returns and sits facing Thomas. Thomas reaches over and pours himself another glass of wine and as he tops up Joan's glass she asks, *"Will you kneel please?"* *"Why?"* demands Thomas. *"What is this about, are we going to have a séance?"* Joan ignores the last question and replies, *"Oh no, it's time to prayer for your soul and our companionship."*

Thomas pointedly replies, *"There is nothing wrong with my soul, and what is this companionship stuff?"* Joan ignores the comment and gestures Thomas to kneel down but instead of kneeling, he gets up from the settee and sits on the edge of a chair with his elbows on the table and his hands supporting his chin. Joan begins her prayer with reference to his lifestyle and his soul. Thomas listens attentively but when Joan refers to *"our companionship"* in her prayers, he mutters, *"I've had enough of this shit, I'm going out,"* and gets up from the table.

Joan has her eyes close, which she always do during prayer and does not lip-read his remark. *"What did you say? Don't you know it is sacrilege to interrupt a prayer session?"* Thomas laughs as he replies, *"I said, I've had enough of this and I'm going out, okay?"* Joan is disappointed, to say the least, and also annoyed that Thomas have violated the sanctity of her sitting room during a prayer session and pleads with him to stay. Joan accepts she cannot restrain him and continues to prayer, *"The Lord bless you and keep you, the Lord make his face to shine upon you and be gracious to you, the Lord lift up his countenance upon you and give you peace."* Thomas feels he can no longer cope with Joan's religious way of life, and departs before the end of the week without saying goodbye.

Thomas drifted from town to town after leaving Joan, eventually returning to his original district.

It wasn't easy for Thomas returning to his original district after being away for such a long time, as some of the older residences were still living in the district and had not forgotten him or his family, in particular, his mother Shirley. One of the original residences was a young woman name Carole Riley. Unlike Thomas, Carole and her mother Pauline were victims of domestic abuse and violence.

A few weeks after returning to the district, Thomas and Carole met whilst travelling on a local bus to one of the nearby towns to look for work. As the months passed, Thomas and Carole met regularly but only as friends.

Contrary to what appears to be popular thinking, the impact of illegal drugs does not rest solely with the user but can and do extend to other family members, as well as others close to the user. Although the problem is prevalent, it does not appear to receive the same degree of attention or exposure. Perhaps the assumption is that only the user is affected.

The use of illegal drugs within a family can and do create other risks, such as the likelihood younger children or siblings will begin using the illegal drugs, and consequently develop a dangerous dependency on the drugs and other substances.

There are also the financial and physical long-term costs to the family, which could be particularly high. This situation encourages some family members to reject, abandon or isolate the user.

The impact on a family coping with the stigma of being associated with an illegal drug user, particularly within an immediate family, can range from anger to shame and disappointment. There is also the presumption among some family members that in a sense, illegal drugs have destroyed the whole family. There is also the problem of denial by the user, which prevents them accessing or taking advantage of the care provisions that are available.

The Meeting

Understanding comes form sharing. Share with me and I'll understand.

Carole was the daughter of Fred and Pauline Riley and the eldest for three children. The relationship between her parents was fraught with domestic abuse and relentless violence but Carole remained in the family home because she felt it was her duty to take care of her brother and sister during Pauline's days of incapacity, particularly after a violent attack by Fred. Carole often contemplated leaving home because of the loneliness she felt and the domestic disruption. She was a quiet person by nature but always appeared subdued and rarely argued with anyone. Those who knew Carole suggested her fathers' aggressive behaviour and controlling attitude were responsible for her appearing low-spirited. From an early age, she regularly witnessed the abuse and violence against Pauline, and frequently heard her sobbing after an attack. There were occasions when Carole found her mother lying barely conscious after one of his violent attacks.

The level of violence mete out by Fred on Pauline, made Carole extremely anxious, so much so that she was afraid to leave the house, fearing that she might find her mother badly injured or even dead when she return home. Everyday she lost concentration for a while during school lessons, and her education suffered because she was frequently absent from school.

Pauline left home when she was nineteen to live with her first boyfriend Vince. Her parents disapproved of the union and were angry when she decided to leave the family home. She wanted to be completely independent of her parents and move to another area to live in a one-bedroom apartment. Pauline did not keep in touch with her parents and relied on Vince for emotional and financial support. Unfortunately, Vince lost his job and was unable to find suitable employment. During the weeks that followed, the relationship became tense; Pauline became depressed and fretted about going home to her parents but she was too embarrassed to contact them. Vince suggested that in order to meet the monthly expenses, he would invite an ex-girlfriend to share the apartment and contribute to the expenses but Pauline suggested he should think again about inviting his ex-girlfriend to share their one bedroom apartment. However, Vince was adamant that his ex-girlfriend should be invited to join them and share the costs. Pauline said it was thoughtless of him and gave him and ultimatum. The ex-girlfriend later moved into the apartment and Pauline moved out.

Pauline had no fixed abode; she had very little money and was vulnerable when she met Fred. Fred was recently divorced, and the father of a two-year-old boy whom he had not seen since the divorce. He remained in the three-bedroom house after the divorce and suggested she live with him as a lodger, however, the relationship soon developed. Pauline was unaware that Fred drank heavily or that his wife left him, taking the child because of his drinking. Fred promised to take care of Pauline but reminded her it was his house and would remain his. He made it clear she must not remove anything from the house, alter anything or bring anything into the house without his agreement. They became engaged, she became pregnant and married each other before Carole was born.

Despite the ferocious assaults by Fred, Pauline refused to report him to the police. Some of her friends were particularly angry with her for accepting the abuse and refusing to take legal action against him. Whenever friends confronted her, Pauline defended her stance with, *"He's only like that after a drink, besides, the children need their father and he always say how sorry he is. Besides, what would happen to us if he were sent down? How will his other son feel knowing his father is in prison? He is still my husband and we have three lovely children together."* However, after a particularly vicious attack, she eventually found the courage to report him to the police. The attack left her with a broken nose, one tooth missing and several others loose.

After that attack on Pauline, Fred left the house to live for a short time with an acquaintance. Fred knew Pauline was hurt but he didn't know how badly. A few weeks later, he returned to apologise for hurting Pauline but she was afraid he would attach her again and refused to let him into the house, however, while he was at the door remonstrating, the police arrived and arrested him. Fred was subsequently sent to prison but instead of Pauline feeling safe knowing he was in prison, she felt guilty and blamed herself for Fred's imprisonment. Several of Pauline's friends blamed her for allowing the violence to continue by not reporting Fred to the police earlier, and other friends deserted her after he was sent to prison.

Pauline suffered a nervous breakdown after years of emotional and physical abuse. Consequently, her health deteriorated rapidly and she died after suffering several strokes. About a year after Pauline's death, Carole felt she could no longer be responsible for the wellbeing of her brother and sister, and was terrified Fred might become more abusive towards her. She agonised for weeks before making the painful decision to leave the family home and live with a family friend name Samantha.

Samantha lived not far from Thomas and knew his family's background.

Carole found it tough adjusting to her new surroundings, and felt guilty leaving her brother and sister at the mercy of their abusive father but she knew leaving home was necessary for her safety and her sanity. She returned to the house several times to collect her belongings but was petrified each time, fearful that Fred might be in the house. Her brother Samuel pleaded with her on several occasions to allow him to stay with her but she refused because there were only two rooms in Samanthas' apartment. Carole was relieved to be away from Fred but she was lonely again. Carole found it difficult to settle in her new surroundings because she assumed the neighbours were staring at her and making derogatory comments about leaving the family home but Samantha helped her to adjust and settle.

A few weeks after moving into Samantha's apartment, Carole began looking in earnest for a job in the area but without success. She wanted to retain her independence and was worried she might be unable to contribute financially to the household expenses. In the days that followed, they were arguments about who bought what, who paid for what and how much. Carole disliked arguing with Samantha, which disturbed her more than not paying her way. Her unintended lack of financial contribution created tension between them and questioned the strength of their friendship. The situation prompted Carole to consider looking for work and other accommodation in another area. Carole discussed her reason for leaving with Samantha, and shortly afterwards, she moved out of the apartment.

Carole had a very determined personality and a strong sense of loyalty. She soon adjusted emotionally after leaving Fred, although she still cared for the wellbeing of her brother and sister, and did not tolerate anyone being abusive or attempting to control or treat her with disrespect. Carole did not readily trust anyone or made friends easily, but once someone had become her friend she remained loyal and supportive. Her education suffered due to frequent absences from school but she was determine to improve her education and job prospects an enrolled at a local college.

Living in a much larger town created different and unfamiliar problems for Carole. She was somewhat naive about the difficulties she might encounter whilst living and working in a larger or major town, assuming she would quickly find a good job and suitable accommodation. However, she found herself moving from one apartment to another and changing jobs several times until someone suggested she registered with an agency that offered work and accommodation, or, alternatively, she should look on the Town Centre Advertising Board under *Vacancies* and under *Apartments of Rent*. Carole did not reject the suggestion but continued looking through the employment section in the local papers and visiting the Job Centre, eventually securing a job as a Personal Assistant (PA) to the Director of a building firm. The wages was sufficient to allow her to rent a suitable and affordable apartment, which she moved into after a couple weeks. As the Director's PA, she travelled to various parts of the country and occasionally staying overnight.

The work was interesting and Carole enjoyed the responsibility that came with the position but she was uncomfortable with the Directors' suggestive and controlling behaviour. She deemed his behaviour inappropriate and refused to submit to his demands. However, because of his persistence, she gave up the job and left the company. Consequently, she was again unemployed and could no longer afford to live in the apartment.

After several unsuccessful attempts to find a job and an affordable apartment, Carole remembered the Advertising Board and went along to check the job and apartment for rent sections. Whilst Carole is looking at the board, a woman approaches from behind and asks, *"Hi yuh, are you looking for a job or accommodation? Are you looking to up-grade or just somewhere to sleep?"* Carole looks around and responds; *"Hi yuh, no, I'm not looking to up-grade, I just want somewhere suitable and affordable."* The woman takes a good look at Carole and continues; *"Are you staying somewhere local?"* Carole turns and looks at the board; *"Yes but I can't afford the one I'm renting. It's a lovely apartment but I'll have to move out soon."*

The woman moves around, faces Carole and introduces herself. *"My name is Bernadette. Are you interested in sharing?"* Carole is quick to reply. *"No, not if I can help it."* Bernadette continues, *"Look, there is a nice little Coffee House over there, let's go for a coffee and a chat about jobs and apartments. I might be able to help you."* Carole turns down the offer at first because she does not know Bernadette. She is determined to find a job and an apartment without any help, particularly from a stranger. However, Bernadette is very persuasive and eventually Carole agrees to the suggestion and accepts the offer of a coffee.

Bernadette lived in the town for more than eight years and knew where the good and not so good apartments were. She also knew where it was dangerous for single women to live and walk, and where women gathered as couples. Bernadette explains, *"It is difficult for women to rent an apartment or get a job around here, especially if they live alone or live together as a couple but I know a woman who runs an outfit who could help you find suitable work."* She also suggests; *"You could move in with me 'til you find a job and a suitable apartment,"* but Carole is uneasy with the suggestion and dismisses it.

Carole did not understand what Bernadette meant by *women living as couples,* or why it was difficult for women living as couples to find an apartment or get a job, and Bernadette did not go into details about relationships or associations among women, nor about the complications that came with women living together. However, she tried convincing Carole that accepting her offer would be beneficial to both of them, and suggests; *"While you're settling in, you can share the basic expenses such as rent, heat and light. The food will be up to you because I don't eat much these days as I'm weight watching—again. At least you would have somewhere to sleep while you're looking for work."*

Carole asks, *"Why are you being so considerate? I've only just met you and know as much about you as you do about me. Sorry, but I can't accept your offer."* Bernadette responds, *"OK, do you want a few days to think it over? Better still, why not come and look at my apartment first, and if you don't like it, you can walk away. Just think of the savings. To be truthful, I could do with some good company, your company. What do you think?"*

Although Carole found the suggestions eerie, especially so early in the association, she was desperate for somewhere affordable to sleep and ponders the idea. She sits up, leans back in her chair and in her boldness, asks; *"Are you a prostitute?"* Bernadette chuckles and replies; *"No, I'm not a prostitute, and there are no prostitutes living near or in my block of apartments."* Carole apologises. *"I'm sorry but I'm not accustomed to such offers of help or generosity. I don't want to appear ungrateful; I don't want to be dependant on anyone except an employer for my wages."*

Carole briefly explained why she left her last job and commented she was determined to prevent anything like that ever happening again. Bernadette listens to Carole but is puzzled by her comment about *"anything like that happening again"* and asks, *"Do you think I'm planning to molest you or make lewd suggestions to you?"* Carole replies; *"No, no, sorry, I didn't mean it in that way, I meant I would not tolerate men behaving like that again."* She reflected on Bernadette's proposals, accepted her offer and moved into the apartment.

Bernadette and Carole became good friends as the weeks passed, sharing experiences, interests and frequenting several bars and nightclubs at the weekend, however, Carole could not understand why only female couples were at the clubs and bars chosen by Bernadette. As the friendship developed, Carole noticed Bernadette becoming possessive, questioning her movements and objecting to her talking to or associating with other women. This observation prompted Carole to ask, *"Bernadette, why are only women in the bars and night clubs we go to, and why are you questioning my movements and objecting to me having friends?"* Bernadette replies, *"You see, I know the clubs, bars and women around here better than you do. It's nothing; I'm only looking out for you."* Carole ponders for a moment before responding. *"Thanks, but I can look out for myself."*

During one of their after dinner chats, Bernadette remarked; *"I think you should share my bedroom. It would reduce the heating and lighting bills. I don't see why we should pay out so much on fuel bills when we don't have to. What do you think?"* Carole replies, *"Although it does make sense, I don't think so, besides, I have never shared a bed with anyone except when I was consoling my mother. I know where you're coming from but I need some time to think about it before making up my mind."* Carole was uneasy about sleeping in the same bed with another woman but thought it would be harmless.

A few weeks later, Carole secured a job as an assistant product sampler at a chemical factory where most of the employees worked part-time. A few employees lived near Bernadette's apartment, except a male employee name Ralph, and travelled to work by public transport. Ralph worked part-time on the section opposite Carole and offered her a lift to work in his car.

Carole was reluctant to accept Ralph's offer because she was worried it would restrict her independence. However, she realised it would be more convenient and less expensive travelling by car and accepted the offer. *"Ok, thanks Ralph but let me give you something towards your petrol."* *"Oh no"*, Ralph replies, *"It's Ok, it will be my pleasure."* Ralph collected her from work as well as from her apartment and soon became collaborates as well as good friends.

During Carole's association with Ralph, the friendship between her and Bernadette became fraught. Bernadette was increasingly inquisitive and controlling, which reminded Carole of Fred's controlling attitude and abusive behaviour. She continually questioned Carole about her friends and about the clubs and bars she visited, suggesting Carole was becoming more popular than she was. Bernadette knew

Carole was an independently minded person and was worried she might leave her apartment to live with someone else if she rebuked or question her too often.

One evening as Carole prepared to leave the apartment to visit Ralph; Bernadette became unusually agitated, pleading with her not to go out that evening. Carole was slightly mystified by her behaviour but instead of cancelling her date with Ralph, she delayed going out until Bernadette explain why she was feeling so insecure. The conversation begun with Bernadette confessing she was in love with Carole. Shocked by Bernadette's confession, Carole asks, *"What do you mean you're in love with me?"*

Bernadette replies. *"I can't help it; I fell in love with you the first time we met at the Ad Board."* As Carole stares at her several questions run through her head. *"Does she hate men? Has her father abused her? Is she a bleeding freak? Am I bloody dreaming?"* Carole breaks her silence and asks Bernadette several questions all at once. *"If you don't have a boy friend, are you a lesbian? Is that why you go to places for women couples only? Is that why you want me to sleep in your bed with you?"*

It is very rarer that Bernadette is challenged, least of all, by the women whom she lures to her apartment. Although it was not the first time she was challenged, this challenge was wholly unexpected. Bernadette takes a few steps back and replies, *"I, I thought you knew that?"* Carole snaps, *"Knew what. What is there to know?"* Bernadette continues, *"I thought you knew I am a lesbian. I have not loved anyone the way I love you. You are attractive, gentle, kind and thoughtful, and I want you to stay, so please, don't go out this evening or with anyone. I can give you whatever you want. You don't have to worry about men or having children. We can have a wonderful life together and we can—,"* Carole interrupts and retorts; *"Look, I like you but I am not a lesbian and I don't want to be a lesbian. I thought a Lesbian was someone who is stupid but you are not, so why are you a lesbian? I want a man to live with as my husband in a proper house, and have children. What makes you think I would want to live with you or have sex with you—a woman?"* Bernadette is unmoved by the rejection and pleads, *"Give it a chance. Give us a chance. We could have nice holidays together and—,"* Carole interrupts again and in a raised voice she exclaims, *"Listen Bernadette, It is not going to happen. I am not in love with you. I like you but I do not love you as a lover. We are not going to be that kind of couple."*

The encounter made Carole extremely apprehensive but she tried desperately not to display her feelings in front of Bernadette.

After composing herself, Carole tells Bernadette, *"I'll move back into the other bedroom and then move out of your apartment as soon as possible. I don't want to hear any more from you about being in love or being a lesbian. You have just ruined our friendship."* Carole took her belongings into the other bedroom and later went out to meet Ralph.

The conversation with Bernadette was still fresh in Carole's mind when she met Ralph but avoided discussing it with him. She felt embarrassed and angry that she had moved in with a self-confessed lesbian, and ashamed she had slept in the same bed, together.

Ralph noticed Carole was particularly sensitive during the evening and, as if he knew something had happened asks, *"Have you fallen out with Bernadette?"* Carole could no longer remain silent and blurts; *"Bernadette is a bloody lesbian and is in love with me and want me to have sex with her. Would you believe it?"* Ralph replies, *"Oh yes, I'm not surprise. Didn't you know she is? Everybody knows."* Ralph continues; *"Bernadette lived with several women in the last year but they all moved out because she treated them badly. According to people who know her, she can be very rough and demanding with her women."*

Carole was taken aback after learning about Bernadette's lifestyle and replies, *"Bernadette was never rough or demanding with me; in fact she was mostly very kind."* She ponders for a moment, stares at Ralph and asks, *"Rough? What do you mean by rough?"* Ralph chuckles, *"They say she likes whipping and being whipped, and sometimes she would have two in a bed. I am surprise you didn't know. Did she pick you up at the Advertising Board on Lesbet Street on the day you were looking for an apartment to rent?"*

Carole was dumfounded. After a few minutes she replies, *"Come to think of it, both her wrists had burn marks as if the wristbands were too tight, and there is a tall narrow cupboard on her side of the bed that is always locked, which she said is used for drying her stockings. Ralph, we are good friends and we like each other, don't we?"* Ralph confirms her observation. *"Yes, I suppose we are but where is this leading? Do you want me to whip you, tie you up, and have sex with you or all three?"* Carole is quick to respond; *"No, no, that's not the reason, at least not the first two,"* and continues; *"Can I move in with you? I will help with the expenses for the apartment—but not the car—and I will sleep in the other room until we both feel it's right to—*she lowers her head as if embarrassed—*you know what I mean."*

Ralph wasn't disappointed Carole didn't want to be rampant with him and replies; *"Yes, I would love that, but don't worry about the sleeping arrangements, I'm not pushy."* Carole is relieved Ralph did not reject her suggestion and continues, *"Thank you, thank you, can I move in with you tomorrow?"* Ralph agrees without hesitation. *"You can move in tonight if you want to but why so soon?"* Carole replies, *"I* have to get out of that apartment quickly otherwise I will hate Bernadette, and I don't want to hate anyone." Carole wasted no time in letting Bernadette know she would be moving out of her apartment at the weekend. Bernadette was infuriated and made it so difficult for Carole; it took her two weeks before she was able to remove all her belongings.

Fred was unremitting in his criticism of Carole. He undermined everything she said and did, and taunted her, *"You will never find anyone to love you. I will make your life a living hell."* He prevented her having friends or mixing with other children, especially with boys older than she was.

On afternoon, Carole was walking home from school with a boy and the boys' sister. Although Fred did not know the children or where they lived, he decided to teach Carole a lesson by embarrassing her in front of them. He raged, *"I told you not to mix with those people. They're not very clean and most of them sleep in the same bed. Is that how you want to live?"* He was so determined to make life difficult for Carole that he cut off the sleeves from one of her shirts, deliberately spilled tomato ketch-up on a pair of her best Jeans and swapped her Gym shorts with a pair of his boxer shorts. Fred also tried to convince her she was too ugly to attract boys or men and would become a lesbian when she grows up. Carole had no idea what a lesbian was at that time and assumed it was someone stupid. She believed she would never find a man who would appreciate, respect or love her because she was stupid.

Despite objections from several family members and those familiar with the way he treated Pauline, Fred returned to the family home after his release from prison. With Pauline's demise still fresh in their memory, some suggested he move to a different town.

About a year after Carole's departure from the family home, Fred suffered a mental breakdown. He was seen in the local park running among the trees exposing himself, and asking, *"Where are you Pauline? I can see you Pauline. I'm coming to get you. I'll get you for this Pauline, I'll get you."* He was apprehended, sectioned and later admitted to a psychiatric hospital.

The friendship between Carole and Ralph grew stronger. He treated her with respect, unlike her father Fred, and allowed her privacy whilst in the apartment. The conversations between them were non-suggestive and mostly about Ralph's friends and his cars. As the weeks passed, Carole became more confident and settled, enough to approach Ralph suggesting she moved into his bedroom. The suggestion was not about saving money; she had grown fond of him and yearned to be closer to him. The suggestion surprised him at first but he remembered Carole mentioned the sleeping arrangements when she first asked if she could move in with him. He liked Carole as a good friend and not as a lover, and did not have any sexual or romantic feelings for her but agreed to her sharing his bed. Carole occasionally tried to be intimate with Ralph but he gently declined her advances.

A few weeks after Carole completed the move into Ralph's apartment, she saw Bernadette loitering near to the Coffee Shop where they first met. Carole was not a person who hated or held grudges against anyone so, although her departure from Bernadette's apartment was somewhat acrimonious, she greeted her politely and offered to buy her a coffee. Bernadette was surprised to see Carole and more so, that she should speak to her but accepted the offer of a coffee.

The Chemical factory lost an important contract and consequently, dismissed several employees from each section. After weeks of uncertainty about her job, coupled with the frustration from a lack of intimacy between her and Ralph, Carole thought it best to separate from Ralph and move back into her bedroom. The words of Fred haunted her making her think it was true she would never find anyone to love her. Carole applied in advance for several jobs in the area but without success. Although she was intelligent, her chances of finding a suitable job were limited because she did not have any of the required academic qualifications.

The Chemical factory eventually dismissed Carole, which increased the uneasiness she felt living with Ralph but he assured her he would not evict her. Nonetheless, Carole was concerned she could not make a full contribution to the expenses and decided to look for other accommodation.

Within two weeks, she found another apartment and moved out of Ralph's apartment. However, finding the apartment was not difficult but keeping up with the rent and meeting the other expenses had become a major concern. She was later forced to move out of that apartment, and reluctantly returned to the family home where she lived for a while with her brother and his partner.

Who Needs Friends?

Friendship occupies your mind, love occupies your heart.

Carole and Thomas lived in the same district for over twelve years but only knew each other as acquaintances. Carole knew nothing of Thomas's family background, the circumstances surrounding his fathers' death nor of the effect the domestic disruption had on him.

The casual acquaintance between them became a serious friendship after moving back to the area, and as they became more relaxed, shared aspects of their past lives with each other. In many respects, they had much in common, except Carole did not smoke, neither did she use or supplied illegal drugs. She drank alcohol but not to excess and admitted she only attended church at Easter, Remembrance Sunday and at Christmas.

Thomas did not confess to Carole he dealt illegal drugs but sought to reassure her that although he was using illegal drugs, he was not addicted, and promised he would stop if they became special friends. Carole understandably assumed his cessation was using drugs, as she knew nothing about his drug-dealing racket.

Thomas and Carole became special friends, he kept his promise and eventually they became partners.

Thomas and Carole enjoyed an active partnership, going places, doing things together, sharing experiences and being supportive of each other, particularly as they had so much in common. Carole recalled Fred's prophecy that she would never find anyone to love her and muttered to herself, *"Fred, you were wrong. I have found someone who loves me."* They were almost inseparable during the early days and decided to consolidate the relationship by announcing their engagement. There were no immediate plans to marry each other but Thomas suggested it should wait until they found suitable accommodation, however, Carole became pregnant before they were married.

The unexpected pregnancy altered their plans but not their desire to marry each other. They both agreed to raise the child in a stable environment and within four months they were married but Carole's family disapproved of her marriage to Thomas and isolated her. Carole was accustomed to coping in stressful situations, so being isolated by her family was just another situation to deal with, however, she realised being pregnant and alone was not a good idea so she reconnected with the few friends she had, Samantha Digby whom she previously stayed with, Gloria Rush and Patricia Fields.

Samantha was the friend with the experience, ideas and advice, who was never afraid to tackle a problem or anyone. Samantha worked for the Prison Service for three years before leaving to pursue a new career. She was nicknamed "Hardsam" by the inmates.

Carole described *Gloria* as her *"short tempered fiery friend."* Gloria always expressed her views and feelings vigorously while waving her finger, gesticulating and rolling her eyes. She normally spoke eloquently but was almost incoherent whenever she became excited.

Patricia was the brain of the trio boasting two "A" levels but appeared to lack basic common sense when it mattered. She once thought it was a good idea to give the dog cough syrup because she thought it was constipated, and was convinced her cloths had shrunk when she begun putting on weight.

Thomas and Carole moved into a three bedroom semi-detached house after they were married and before the birth of their first child. The house was located in a quiet cul-de-sac but the responsibility of married life, fatherhood and running a home begun to impact on Thomas soon after moving to the new home. He refused to cooperate around the house and criticised most of her efforts—including her culinary skills. Thomas became verbally abusive and frequently threatened to abandon her to the mercy of her family, knowing they would reject her again. Although Carole was capable of verbally defending herself, she was neither aggressive nor argumentative and therefore did not confront him about his changed attitude towards her.

The sudden and unexpected change in his behaviour mystified her. She was unaware of his past aggression.

Unknown to Carole, Thomas returned to the habits he promised to stop if they became special friends. He often left home without saying where he was going or when he would return but when Carole asked him where he was or with whom he ranted and raged.

The Turning Point

Most people walk in and out of your life but friends leave footprints in your heart.

The verbal abuse, threats and foul language intensified after Carole suggested he cleaned his teeth. The suggestion sent him into a furious rage, gesticulating, banging the table and ranting, *"So you think you can fucking insult me by saying I have bad breath and dirty teeth. What I put in my mouth or what I eat has fuckall to do with you. How do you know it's not that shit you give me? Why don't you—"* Carole interrupts, *"Thomas, Thomas, I wasn't trying to insult you but your breath has never smelled like that. What is it? Is it something you—?"* Thomas snaps, *"Shut up, just shut up you stupid bitch, you don't know anything, fucking shut up. I am warning you, if you attempt to insult me again I will kick your arse through that door. I've had enough of you. I'm going out and I don't want to come back to anymore of that shit. I want proper food. You should learn to cook like Joan did."* Thomas had never mentioned Joan so, naturally, Carole wanted to know about Joan and asks, *"Who is Joan?"* Thomas replies, *"Never mind, in any case she was better than you will ever be—a proper cook, cooking proper food."* Carole wasn't jealous but felt belittled

72

by the comparison. It reminded her of her the times Fred humiliated her in front of her friends.

Thomas' attitude and behaviour changed from the thoughtful, understanding and caring friend to an angry, abusive and disrespectful husband and father to be. He frequently berated her in public and accused her of flirting with other men whenever she or they were out walking or shopping.

On one occasion, during a drunken frenzy, he threatened Carole; *"I'll knock that thing out of you and shove it down your fucking throat,"* after which he slapped her face but not hard enough to knock her out or cause injury to their unborn child. This was his first physical abuse of the marriage. Three months later, Carole gave birth to a baby girl whom they named *Jamie*.

Soon after *Jamie* was born, Thomas increased his drug use and drug-dealing racket. He frequently lost his temper, he became more verbally abusive, sexually demanding and sometimes he prevented her from leaving the house for up to four days. Occasionally he refused to hand over money for house keeping without any consideration of the difficulty Carole would have in meeting the household needs. Eventually he took full control of the finances but allowed her enough money to cater for the basic needs each week, including baby essentials and used the remainder to buy alcohol and illegal drugs. He refused to help Carole clean, feed or comfort Jamie during the night but complained the child woke him up during the night and kept him awake. There were times when he suggested Carole; *"Make that thing shut up or put it outside. I want to get some fucking sleep."* He regularly reminded Carole, *"I earn the fucking money around here. It's your job to look after that."*

Thomas insisted Carole did not invite her friends to visit her at home and warned her against contacting them via the house telephone but whenever she disobeyed him, he punished her. Carole's punishment ranged from withholding the house keeping, to verbal humiliation in front of his friends. However, the physical punishment only took place after his friends leave the house and before Jamie or James arrives home. Carole protested it was unreasonable that he should deny her the company of her friends whilst inviting his friends to the house, and insisting she waited on them but her protests made no difference. She felt undermined and demoralised since she neither spoke to nor associated with his friends.

Whenever Thomas wanted a supply of drugs, he openly revisited women clients whom he met as courier for Theresa. The friends that remained loyal to Carole took it in turn to visit her at home to take care of Jamie whilst she rested, but as soon as Thomas arrive home, he would intimidate whoever it was, he would be sarcastic, rude and generally disruptive. His behaviour was humiliating and obnoxious but it did not deter them from visiting her. They were determined to continue supporting Carole and met regularly at previously arranged locations and secretly at the house. Her friends also kept in touch by telephone, which angered Thomas. During one of his outbursts he threatened; *"I'll rip that fucking telephone out of its socket and throw it in the fucking bin if you don't stop telephoning those other bitches,"* and demanded she stop all contact by telephone.

As the weeks passed, he took advantage of her vulnerability, intensified his emotional and verbal abuse, and disallowed her contact with her friends by whatever means.

Thomas was sure he had succeeded in totally isolating Carole from family and friends but she continued to have regular visits from Samantha, Gloria and Patricia, albeit in secret.

During Carole's' isolation, the violence escalated becoming more physical, particularly after he returned from one of his overnight jaunts with his newfound friends. Carole was apprehensive about the intensity of the abuse as it reminded her of the violence Fred inflicted upon Pauline, which contributed to her death. However, she assumed the violence would lessen as Jamie grew older but remembered Fred intensified his violence against Pauline before she became a teenager.

Friendship can survive without love but love cannot survive without friendship.

Samantha Rigby is one of Caroles' loyal friends and is aware that the abuse is worsening, but despite numerous warnings from Samantha, Gloria and Patricia that Thomas is likely to inflict a serious injury on her, Carole refuses to report the abuse and remains in the abusive relationship.

Samantha arrives just after midday on one of her secret home visits, and finds Carole is still in her dressing gown. This is an unusual shift from her smart appearance for the time of day. None of her friends arrives before midday in case Thomas is at home. The visits usually last a couple of hours and in any case before the children arrive home from school because there is always the risk Jamie or James innocently revealing to Thomas *"Mums' friend was at the house today."* She notices Carole is swaying and dragging one foot with her legs open as she walks across the room, as if she recently ridden or fallen from a horse. Samantha also notices how uncomfortable Carole appears as she sits down, struggles to position herself onto the chair and holds her stomach.

Carole always gave Samantha, as well as the other girls, a vivacious welcome but on this occasion, she is unusually quiet for the first five minutes. The observation prompts Samantha to ask, *"Are you feeling unwell Carole?"* Carole is slow to respond and slurs her words as she does so. *"I don't feel very well, my head hurts, my stomach hurts, my leg hurts, my arse hurts and my fairy hurts. What isn't swollen is bruised. Everywhere and everything hurts."*

Carole always updates her friends on the latest abuse but Samantha has never seen her in such a beaten-up condition and anxiously asks, *"What is wrong with you? You look terrible. Have you fallen and hurt yourself? Has Thomas done this to you?"* Carole makes herself as comfortable as possible and asks Samantha; *"Would you bring me a glass of water please?"* This gave her time to make another adjustment before Samantha return with the water.

Samantha thinks Carole should have something different and asks, *"Would you prefer a cup of tea or something stronger?"* but Carole is insistent, *"No, no, just a glass of water please and I'll tell you what happened."*

Carole begins; *"Thomas came home from wherever, had his dinner, which he said was home cooked shit, and went out again but came back later than I expected him to. I didn't have a time in mind but he is not usually too late coming home so I was a little worried. I was lying on top of the bed when he came in, so I got up and, out of concern, asked why he was so late and why his breath smelled so sickly. I stopped kissing him months ago because his breath stinks of something he drinks or eats. I told him I was worried and that I was going to check with the hospital in case he had an accident or something."*

Carole pauses to catch her breath, repositions herself to ease the pain, and continues; *"He pushed me to one side, told me to bloody shut up or he would give me a thick lip. He said it wasn't any of my fucking business where he was, who he was with or what he did."* She pauses again, alters her position on the chair and continues. *"I told him I wasn't checking on him or anything like that but he became angrier, he came towards me with his fist clenched but turned away and said it was my last fucking warning. I asked him not to shout or use bad language in case Jamie is awake"*

Carole pauses again for breath, takes another sip of water and continues. *"After checking if Jaime is asleep, he came back to me and without saying anything, slapped the side of my head so hard I saw stars. The stars looked like planets. As I stumbled backwards, I asked him why he did that but he stared at me, muttered something and kicked me between my legs. I begged him not to kick me there again but he threatened to do it harder if I didn't shut up and stop asking questions. I was sure he would kick me there again so I kept quiet. I couldn't keep my balance, my head was hurting, I was swollen and sore down there, and my stomach was hurting so badly I wanted to pass-out but I had to prevent myself falling in case he kicked me there again."*

Samantha interrupts, *"You should get out of here, leave now, once and for all because one day that bastard will kill you. In fact, he is killing you now, and I think you know it. Why are you putting up with this brutality? What will you do when he cripples you?"* Carole replies as if she is sure she knows how Thomas feels and why he reacts the way he does. *"I think he was drunk and probably didn't realise what he was doing at that time so I—"* Samantha quickly interrupts again; *"He knew what he was doing because he made sure Jaime was asleep before he started on you. One day, one day he will kill you, I know he will. You should get out now."*

Carole is quick to defend Thomas and reminds Samantha, *"Samantha, you, Patricia and Gloria are my friends but you don't know Thomas like I do. You don't know what his mother did to him, besides, he is a good father to Jamie and I don't want her growing up not knowing her father like—,"* Samantha sharply interrupts, *"And what about Jamie growing up without knowing her good mother. Have you thought of her?"* Carole pauses for breath before replying. *"I'm worried. I am very worried because he is becoming more vicious with me, although, I don't think it will come to that. I don't think he will kill anyone."* Samantha replies, *"No, you're right, not anyone, just you."*

Samantha recalls with Carole, *"How many times have you been to A & E as a walk-in patient and by Ambulance as an emergency? How many times have you asked me to come over because you thought Thomas had broken one of your arms? How many times have you hidden the bruises from Jamie? How many times have you said he is going to kill you? You may have forgotten but I haven't, and if you don't want him to cripple or kill you, you have to leave and take Jamie with you."*

Carole ponders over Samantha's last comment between repositioning herself on the chair and asks, *"Where could I go? I cannot go to my family because they don't want to know me. You and the other girls live too close to us so Thomas would easily find us, besides, how would I get our things together without him knowing or catching us? I don't know what to do. I only have you three to turn to"* Carole pauses, takes a deep and painful breath and asks, *"Could you get another drink for me please?"*

It is nearly time to leave the house and Samantha is in a dilemma. She agonizes about the decision she is about to make as she prepares the drink for Carole. She mumbles to herself, *"If I'm in the house when Thomas arrives, he might not say anything to me but later the bastard will give her a bloody good hiding. If I leave her in that condition, she might not go to A & E. She is my friend and she needs me now so I'm staying with her, whatever that bastard thinks or says, I'm staying."*

Samantha decides it is time she stand up to Thomas but knows standing up to him at that time will not be in Carole's best interest and could have serious repercussions, putting her safety or even her life at risk but Samantha chooses to stay, confront Thomas and if necessary, try to calm the situation.

Samantha returns to Carole with the drink and promptly announces her decision. *"Right, I've been thinking, we've been friends long before Thomas came along. I know what you have been through with your mum and dad, and now the rest of the family don't want to know you but I am not walking away from you now that you could do with a little extra support. I don't know why you put up with that bastard, even if he is your husband. So, I've decided to stay until you go to A & E or 'till Thomas comes home."*

Carole straightens up as best she could, winces as she rubs her stomach and panics after Samantha delivers her decision. She raises her voice, *"It's not a good idea. You have to leave. No, you must go now before they come. I know you mean well but think of what he might do and how Jamie will feel if she sees her dad being angry with me. Please, I don't want to go through this again. If you are my friend you will understand what I'm saying and leave now. The idea is making me feel more sick."*

**When I listen to my head, it tells me what I must
do. When I listen to my heart it tells me how I am
feeling.**

Carole pauses, holds the side of her head and continues.
*"I don't know what to do and now I'm confused. I'm in so
much bloody pain. What should I do?"* She cries but there
are no tears. *"I don't want you to leave but I'm too frightened
to let you stay because I know Thomas will be bloody angry
if he sees you. I have to start preparing his and Jamie's dinner
because it's getting late. You are not supposed to be here. He
doesn't know—,"* Samantha interrupts, *"I know but what are
friends for when you need them?"* Carole continues, *"How
will I explain why you're here? He will not believe anything
I say. Maybe I can say—,"* Samantha interrupts again, *"You
don't have to say anything, I will do the talking for both of us.
Don't worry, I'm not going to say or do anything to antagonise
him or upset Jamie, but if he starts on me, I'll, never mind, I'll
just wait 'till the bastard gets here."*

Samantha positions the chair so that she could see
Thomas and Jamie as they enter the hallway, and so that
Thomas could see her before he sees Carole. Carole shrikes
*"Samantha, what are you doing? I don't have the chair facing
the door. He will know there is something wrong as soon as
he sees it."* Samantha explains that with the chair in that
position, Thomas would see her first, which would give
him time to think of something to direct at her. Carole is
not convince the plan will work but accepts she is not in a
position to argue.

In a study of some two hundred women who had
experienced domestic violence, over 50% of the women
parted company with their abuser because they feared for
their life and the life of their children. Most of the women

who contemplated separating from their abusive partner did so because they suffered relentless abuse, which varied from verbal and emotional to serious threats against them and their children, including physical violence and sexual abuse.

The threat of ending an abusive relationship does not prevent further abuse, or stop the existing abuse but appears to fuel the intensity of the abuse, especially where there is an arrangement for child contact. The risk to the victim appears to increase either at the time of separation, or sometime soon after the separation.

Where there is inadequate protection or support for the victims, the perpetrators take advantage of their isolation and vulnerability, which all too frequently culminates in the victims' death.

In 2001, it was reported that on average, two women were killed each week by their respective violent partner, and that over 40% of females who died because of domestic violence, were killed by the partner with whom they were living or by a former partner, compared with fewer than 5% of male victims.

Samantha suspects Carole is not telling her everything about the battering and asks, *"Is that all that happened? Is there something else? I think there is. I can see bruising behind your left ear. Is that dried blood on your ear lobe?"* Carole struggles to stay awake and several times asks Samantha to repeat a question or a comment.

Carole continues, *"I felt dizzy and loosing my balance so I sat on the edge of the bed. He came behind me, grabbed my hair and pulled me backwards onto the bed. I felt too dizzy to move so I stayed in that position. He then pulled up my dressing gown, spread my legs apart and said he is going to give me what I'm asking for. I told him I wasn't asking for anything and that I was only lying on my back because he had pulled me backwards. I told him that I was swollen down there and hurting badly, and asked him to wait until the morning but he ignored me and—"* Carole stops talking, rubs her stomach and changes her sitting position to ease the pain.

Samantha allows Carole a little time to recover before asking, *"Did he rape you? Did Thomas rape you? Did he? Oh-my-God."* Carole hesitates then replies; *"He was rough with me and afterwards, he kicked my leg and told me to get up and clean myself but I felt sick and too exhausted to move. He then grabbed the collar of my dressing gown and pulled me up. I couldn't see properly so I reached for the dressing table but before I could get my balance, he punched me to the side of my head knocking me against the wall. I bounced off the wall and onto the corner of the dressing table and collapsed onto the floor."*

Samantha comments, *"So he did rape you and hit you, and that's why there's bruising behind your ear. Have you been bleeding from your ear?"* Carole winces before replying. *"I think so. I don't know. I saw blood on my face towel but I didn't think it was coming from inside my ear. Is it very bad?"*

> **Time is not always a healer. Time will only be a healer if the wound can be healed.**

Bleeding from the ear gives notice of a very serious disorder, which might be caused by a life-threatening condition such as Cancer of the ear, head trauma from a heavy blow to the head, trauma to the ear canal or middle ear or from a hard slap. Bleeding from the ear due to a blow to the head could be life threatening because serious complications could develop leading to permanent brain damage. Other reasons for bleeding from the ear include a ruptured or perforated eardrum, which is another cause for concern, as it is a natural barrier to germs entering the middle and inner ear. Such a condition should not be ignored, assuming it will go away, or that it will not develop but it should be investigated immediately, at least as an emergency.

A head injury can occur in a variety of circumstances, for example; a road accident, rock climbing, mountaineering, boxing and other contact sports, slip, trip or diving. However, head injuries are frequently dismissed, especially by the victim, but should be taken seriously and be investigated. A head injuries may occur in an area such as the scalp, skull and may cause a minor headache at that time, which may or may not be associated with brain injury. However, it is understood that if bleeding occurs with-in the skull, a build up of blood can put pressure on the brain, which can be fatal.

Samantha insists, *"It doesn't mater how bad it is, you shouldn't put up with this any longer. Either you go to A & E now or go to the police because—."* Carole interrupts, her voice portrays utter panic as she pleads with Samantha, *"No, no, please, not the police, I don't want to go to the police and I don't want you to call them. If you call the police, Thomas might leave me and take Jamie with him. He says I am not a good mother and that I cannot do anything right. I'm not a bad mother, am I? Do you think I am? I'll go to A & E if you promise not to call the police."*

Samantha replies, *"Carole, It's up to you what you do first but I think you should call the police and report this attack. At the very least, go to A & E, especially with that bleeding ear, I mean with blood coming from your ear. Would you like me to go with you? On second thoughts, I think you should send for an Ambulance because it looks too serious to go by Taxi, besides, you can be there and back before he comes in. What do you want me to do?"* Although Carole wants to go to A & E, she is worried the hospital might not discharge her after treatment. She have not experience such pain or discomfort before, and is afraid her injuries might be severe enough for the hospital to keep her in for more than a day, or have her transferred to another hospital to be treated for her head injury.

Carole looks at Samantha for a while before answering. *"I know you're looking out for me, and I know I should go to the A & E but it's getting late and Jamie will be home soon. I don't want her to come home to an empty house because she will be worried about me. I'm always here when she comes home and her dinner is always ready. My ear is not bleeding and I'm only a little stiff. Resting now you are here helped, so I'll take a couple painkillers."*

A good woman may not become a good wife, but a good wife is a good woman.

Thomas never leaves the house without breakfast, unless it was one of his early afternoons' lie-in but whatever the reason or occasion, Carole had to prepare the meal. She never knew what he wanted until the last minute and he often changed his mind whilst she was preparing what he first asked for, and sometimes what he asked for the second time. Meal time, in particular Breakfast time, was always a stressful time for Carole, because whatever Thomas asks for, she had to be ready to prepare something different within the same period as well as get it right.

One morning, Thomas demanded toast and coffee for his breakfast, which Carole prepared and, as usual, took it to the table soon after he sat down. She then returned to the kitchen to prepare Jamie's breakfast. Thomas stared at the toast intensely before complaining that an edge on one side was too dark, the butter was unevenly spread and that the coffee was not sweet enough despite instructing Carole not to put sugar in his coffee. Without thinking of the consequences for arguing or challenging him, Carole remarks, *"Thomas, there's nothing wrong with the toast, and you said you didn't want any sugar in your coffee. I'll make you another slice in a minute. Do you want sugar in your coffee?"*

Thomas does not tolerate dissent at best, so when Carole challenged him, he becomes enraged. He gets up from the table like grease lighting; kicks open the kitchen door and rushes towards her. Carole is facing the sink and doesn't turn 'round before Thomas reaches her; he grabs her around the throat from behind, pushes her face into the sink bowl and pulls her backwards by the hair to the dining table. Carole struggles to breathe after near strangulation and drowning as Thomas pushes her face onto the toast, repeating, *"You useless bitch. You useless bitch, what's this shit?"* Carole is still finding it difficult to breathe and cannot respond quickly but Thomas Ignores her immediate discomfort, and strikes her on the side of the head. She staggers backwards from the force of the blow and collides with a wall unit but manages to maintain her balance and remains on her feet. She is dazed and struggles to maintain her balance as she turns away pleading with Thomas, *"Please, stop, you are hurting me. Jamie is coming down and I don't want her to see me like this. I'll make it again the way you want it. You sit down and I'll bring it to you."*

As usual, Thomas ignores her pleas and her compromise. He comments, *"What? You want to give me more of that shit. If you can't get it right first time, there's little chance a useless bitch like you getting it right second time,"* and kicks the back of her legs with such force; it sent her sprawling onto the kitchen floor. As Carole struggles to get up, he grabs her dressing gown, pulls her back into the dining area, pushes her against the wall and slaps the side of her head with the back of his hand. The force of the blow knocks her onto the narrow edge of the table but as she clings to the table, Thomas kicks her feet from under her. She struggles to hold on but looses her balance and strikes her head against the edge of the table as she falls to the floor.

Carole is stunned but conscious as she lies on her back under the table. Her dressing gown is partly open exposing her breasts and vagina. She raises her hands in submission and pleads with Thomas, *"Don't hurt me anymore. Please, help me up before Jamie come down. I don't want her to see me like this. Please Thomas please,"* but he ignores her pleas. Thomas is sexually stimulated at the sight of Carols' exposed breasts and vagina, and instead of helping her to get up, he taunts her with comments such as, *"Ah hah, you're ready for it again, get up you bitch or I'll give it to you right here. Get up, get up you useless bitch, I said get to fuck up."* In the end, he grabs her outstretched hand and, as he pulls her up, she winces but it makes no difference to Thomas. He pulls her across the room, pushes her onto the settee and forcefully has sexual intercourse with her. After the act he snarls, *"Get up and clean yourself. Come on, get up."* Carole does not go upstairs in case Jamie sees her and asks why she was in the bathroom but goes back to the kitchen and prepares Jamie's breakfast.

Samantha knows Thomas is violent with Carole and that she regularly attends A & E for treatment but is shocked at the level of violence on this occasion and decides she will ask Patricia and Gloria to come to the house for added support. Carole pleads with Samantha, *"Oh no, please, don't.*

It will make Thomas angry with me if he comes in and see all three of you here. I know Gloria will shout at him and I don't want that. I'll go to A &—" Samantha interrupts, *"You said you only need painkillers, so why have you changed your mind about going to A & E? Is it so that we won't be here when he comes in? If you want to go to A & E, one of us will go with you but Thomas has to be told he cannot continue abusing you and get way with it."* Carole replies, *"He will be OK if it is only me and Jamie. If Gloria says anything to him, he may not do anything, besides he will have Jamie with him but afterwards he will start again, I know he will. Oh please, do as I ask just this once please."* Samantha agrees, with reluctance, but reminds Carole; *"If we see you like this again—if you're not dead, we' will confront him. I'm leaving but I will tell the girls about this. OK, It's nearly time for Jamie, so I'll go before he comes in. We'll come and see you later this week and you will see us—if you're not dead."*

Jamie did not witness the physical abuse against Carole in her early years but she frequently heard the verbal abuse. The abuse was not always shouting and banging, it included sarcasm, insults, condemnations and a barrage of humiliating comments in her presence. On one occasion, Carole and Jamie were sitting together on the settee when Thomas remarked, *"Jamie I hope you don't grow up to be a stupid lazy cow like this one here."* Jamie caught a glimpse of Carole's sad expression and moved closer as if to comfort her.

Thomas incessant criticism of the meals Carole prepared had a dramatic effect on Jamie. Jamie begun refusing certain foods she previously liked because Thomas gave her the impression that the food was not fit to eat. This created some confusion with Jamie because some of the meals Carole prepared at home were included as school meals.

The relationship between Jamie and her parents was never in doubt. Jamie was never made to feel she was responsible for her parents' disagreements. Thomas and Carole—particularly Carole, always made sure Jamie was not in the room or away from the immediate area during an argument. This resulted in Jamie spending long periods alone in her room.

During her early years, Jamie was rarely seen with her parents and this continued when she was old enough to make her way to school. Jamie did not question Thomas about the verbal abuse but often say to Carole, *"When Dad wakes me up I can't get back to sleep. Why can't I come into your room?"* On several occasions Jamie would ask Carole, *"Mummy, Is your face hurting?"* or, *"Mummy, is your bum sore?"* or, *"Is Daddy angry with me as well?"*

Once Jamie was old enough to attend school by herself, Thomas would often stay in bed untill early afternoon, except Saturdays. Saturday was the day he made an effort to take Jamie on *outings* such as the cinema, a fairground or a fast food restaurant. After getting up in the afternoon, he would demand Carole prepare his dinner before Jamie arrive home from school, because he objected to having his meals at the same time as Carole and Jamie. Carole was always under pressure to meet his demands and have his meals ready at a certain time, whilst catering for Jamie when she arrives home, unless there was an after-school activity.

One morning soon after Jamie left the house, Thomas announced in a somewhat disrespectful and abusive tone, *"Look you, I'm going out and I won't be back for about three days, so you better be fucking here when I get back, and I don't want anyone else in my fucking house when I'm away. You know who I'm talking about."* The idea of three days without abuse or violence appealed to Carole but she was apprehensive and became very anxious. Thomas frequently went away without telling her why or where he was going but always return the same day refusing to say where he was. He had never stayed away for such a long time and Carole had no idea where he was likely to be for such a long time, with whom or why and she dared not ask. She was particularly concerned that Jamie might be worried if Thomas was not at home when she arrives, and more so, because she will not have any answers concerning his whereabouts.

Carole was cautious not to display any signs of elation or pleasure about his intended absence but saw it as a chance to meet her friends and have a good chat about herself and her future with Thomas. On the other hand, she didn't want to appear careless about his welfare and tried to show her concern by asking, *"Thomas, do you want me to make your breakfast first or put up something for you to take with you?"* Thomas grunts, *"No, I don't want any of that shit from you. I'll get some proper food when I'm out, and before you ask, it's fuck-all to do with you where I'm going, just make sure you're fucking home alone with the Kid when I get back."* Carole knows Jamie will be worried and asks, *"If you are going to be away for such a long time, what do I tell Jamie?"* Without hesitation, Thomas responds *"Tell her, tell her fuckall. Look, you think of something if you have the brains to, you think of something. You're always asking questions, how about finding some answers? I'm going away and that's all you need to know."*

Thomas did not associate with his next-door neighbours or any of the other residents, and several of his original friends deserted him after he moved into the house. However, during the previous months he made new like-minded friends, all of whom smoked, drank heavily and used illegal drugs, and began meeting and staying out regularly.

Carole knew he used illegal drugs before they became friends, and feared his new friends might encourage him to indulge more often thus becoming addicted.

Carole was unfamiliar with the description or full effects of illegal drugs, so when it appeared, or she suspected Thomas had taken drugs, she was unable to identify what it was or how much he might have taken and certainly not the source. She noticed his behaviour changed on certain days but she had no idea whom he met or what he took on that day. She also noticed there were certain days when he was particularly amorous, suggesting she create a romantic setting with candles, wine, music and drawn curtains. Carole loved the setting but he would then demand sexual intercourse several times during the romantic setting, and talked about seeing beautiful colours although nothing had changed at that time in the dimly lit room. The frequency of sexual intercourse made her feel uncomfortable and used but she lacked the courage to protest. However, as soon as the romantic condition had worn off he returned to his violent and abusive ways.

There were other times he appeared restless, full of energy and boasting he could do anything he set his mind to but did nothing to help around the house. Other times he appeared somewhat lethargic, depressed and impotent. On occasions, he rubbed his nose continuously and complained that his nostrils were either blocked or sore but when Carole suggested something to unblock his nostrils; he quickly became verbally aggressive and ranted incoherently.

One evening, Thomas arrived home looking as if he had just woken from a very bad dream. Carole was worried that a drug dealer or someone high on drugs might have threatened him. He was never short of money but she wondered if he were thinking about the beating he would receive if he did not pay for his drugs. She knows he would erupt in a fit of rage if she appears too inquisitive all at once about his experience, and decides to question him at intervals. While she is cautiously weighing him up, Thomas looks at her as if she is invisible.

The colour is rapidly draining from his face; he is trembling and appears more anxious than usual. Carole takes a chance, even though she is standing about eight feet away from him and asks, *"Thomas, Thomas, did, did someone, did someone threatened you?"* Thomas snaps, *"What the fuck is it to do with you?"* She waits a few minutes and asks, *"Have you taken something you shouldn't?"* Thomas snaps again, *"Look, I said it's fuck-all to do with you what I take or where I got it from, just keep your bloody nose out or I'll break it."*

Carole usually avoids challenging or contradicting Thomas but something he said invoks her determination to ask more questions. She moves closer to him whilst remaining at a safe distance and continues. *"I didn't ask you who or where you got anything from, or when you took it. But did you get it from a stranger or from someone you know?"* Thomas is impatient, angrier and is struggling to breath but wants to maintain control of the situation. He turns to Carole and menacingly shouts as he bangs the table, *"Questions, questions, questions, all you do is ask fucking questions. Can't you see I've had a—"* he pauses, stops banging the table and looks away. Carole persists and asks, *"What have you had?"* He stares at Carole, and, as if in submission to her persistence replies, *"LSD tablet. I took an LSD tablet. One fucking LSD tablet. Are you happy now?"*

Carole remembers Pauline talking to her about LSD but said it meant Pounds Shillings and Pence—something to do with "old money." Carole knows nothing about the drug LSD, its' affects or how long its affects lasts. She is familiar with the name of some drugs such as Heroin and Cocaine but has no idea how the user reacts after taking the drugs. She is not interested in the name of the drug at that time but is worried that Thomas might be in serious danger after taking the LSD tablet. She moves a little closer to him and asks, *"What has it done to you? Please, tell me so that I know what do if you look like this again."* He is reluctant but for the first time submissively shares his experience.

Thomas begins; *"I took one LSD tablet this morning and by lunch time it started to work. I felt something rushing through my body, more so in my back, and my stomach felt weird. I didn't want to go out, as you know, even though it was sunny but I desperately wanted to go for a walk. I didn't have anywhere in mind, it was as if I was being carried away. I felt a little uncomfortable but thought it would be best to wait 'till whatever was happening to me ware off or settle down.*

*I could see lots of pretty patterns all over my body but I couldn't feel anything moving. Everyone I met had an extra limb and several eyes. I strolled into the park to sit for a few minutes but found myself crawling on the grass looking at enormous insects the size of Turkeys. They had very big blue and red eyes and wearing crash helmets with the letters **C** at the front and **J** at the back.*

I tried to catch them but they kept running away and surrounding me. One took off its helmet and tried to grab my balls but I kicked it away, and as I got up to make my way home, other creatures that look like snakes with legs started following me. I was frighten and confused, and didn't know which way to the house or shops. One of the creatures said something but I could not understand it. The creatures slithered behind me all the way home but when I tried to stamping on them, some disappeared and others got smaller but I managed to leave them at the door.

When I came into the house and saw you, you looked so disfigured; I thought you were one of them so I was going to kill you. That's it. Now that you know stop asking so many fucking questions." Carole persists and asks, *"What can I get you? What do you want me to do?"* Thomas turns, stares at her for a few seconds and replies, *"Fuck off, you've asked enough questions, that's what you can do."*

Whenever Thomas returned home after staying away longer than a day, he became more physically abusive. Some of Caroles' injuries were severe enough for her to remain in Hospital overnight but still she refused to report the abuse to the police, fearing she might loose Jamie. Four years after Jamie was born, Carole became pregnant and gave birth to their second child, a boy, whom they named *James*.

Jamie had become accustomed to the shouting between Carole and Thomas but only became aware of the violence as she got older. Jamie did not go to her parents during the violence but stayed in her room or moved into another room. Sometimes she went out of the house but didn't go very far. However, her curiosity was developing sufficient to ask Carole more questions such as:

"Mum, why do you go to hospital so often?"

"Why are you always upsetting Dad? Is it because you have to go to the hospital?"

"Why is your hand always bandaged?"

"Why are you always crying?"

"Why do you upset Dad?"

"Why does Dad go way so often?"

There is a general assumption that children who witness domestic abuse are likely to be either abusers or victims of abuse later in their lives. Unfortunately, boys learn from their abusive fathers or male adults to be violent against women and girls learn from their mothers or other female adults that violence is to be expected and accepted.

However, not every child that witness domestic abuse will become abusers or victims of abuse. In many situations, boys grow up endeavouring to behave diffidently, unlike the male abuser and girls grow up determine not to make the same mistakes as their female victims.

Carole replies, *"Sometimes your Dad gets very upset but it's not always me that upsets him, or that he is upset with."* Jamie quickly reminds Carole, *"But Mum, whenever I upset you, you shout at me and smack my hand or the back of my leg, so you must be upsetting Dad for him to shout at you or smack you. Why do you cry so often? Is it because you are always hurting your arm?"* Carole continues, *"Your Dad says he loves me, he loves you and he loves James but he doesn't always feel happy. Something happened when he was with his family, long before you were born, and it upsets him when he thinks about it. He doesn't always want to think or talk about it because when he does, it upsets him and he finds it difficult to calm down."*

Jamie asks, *"Will my Dad get upset with me and James as well? Will we have to go to the hospital afterwards?"* Carole replies, *"No, no, it's not like that, your Dad wouldn't do anything to make you or James go to the hospital."* Jamie continues, *"Does my Dad take drugs? My friend says her Dad takes drugs and that he is always asleep but he doesn't send her mum to hospital or hurt her hand. Mum, what is a smackhead?"*

Carole found it difficult to contain the whole truth about Thomas but she reassured Jamie that her Dad is not a drug addict, and that neither she nor James would be going to hospital if Thomas got upset with either of them.

Thomas became more ruthless as Jamie grew older and showed little concern for her emotional wellbeing. During her early years, he made an effort to exclude her when an argument erupted between him and Carole, now he does not hesitate to be verbally abusive in her presence. There were occasions when Jamie urinated before reaching the bathroom, because she was so distressed after witnessing the abuse against Carole. Her concentration lapses, her schoolwork suffered and she started bed-wetting again. Jamie became more anxious between leaving home in the morning and returning home after school, fearing that Carole might be lying somewhere in the house badly injured.

Jamie did not understand the meaning of domestic abuse but was usually the one to express sympathy with Carole. James wasn't unsympathetic but from an early age, Thomas discouraged him from demonstrating his feelings, even to his mother. Thomas once remarked, *"I want my son to be a Tiger when he grows up not a bloody fairy."*

James once asked Jamie, *"Why is Dad always shouting at our mum?"* Jamie could not find an answer easy for James to understand because she does not fully understand; besides she doesn't want to take sides and replies, *"Dad loves my Mum, he loves me and he loves you, so shurrup asking so many questions."* James was discouraged from asking any more questions and accepted the explanation, especially since he knew his Dad loved him, Jamie and his Mum.

The abuse against Carole did not affect James as it did Jamie because to him, that kind of behaviour was to be expected at home, furthermore, it was what he had become accustomed. James loved his mother and his father, and knew they both loved him, so to him the behaviour had a sense of normality.

Thomas arrives home unexpectedly from one of his overnight juants, and after checking that Jamie and James are asleep, unleashes his aggression on Carole. Carole is not expecting him to arrive home at that time, so she has not prepared the usual welcome. She breaks her routine and spends the evening with Jamie and James instead of rushing from room to room tidying up to appease him. The assumption is, had he arrive home an hour later, he might not have been too disappointed. However, that assumption might not be justified because he would find another reason for reprimanding her. On this occasion, neither Jamie nor James is asleep.

The Ambulance Service, medical staff at the District Hospital and those in A & E knew Carole. She all too frequently called the Ambulance, which took her to A & E but despite the frequency and severity of the violence, she refused to press charges against Thomas.

The beating was so severe Carole had to remain in hospital overnight. Her injuries are not life threatening at that time but the warnings from her friends about her safety returned to haunt her after that attack.

Carole gave Samantha, Gloria and Patricia the full details about the night of violence during their secret visit, and decided she will leave Thomas and take the children with her. However, Samantha reminds her, *"Look, you have no family to assist or support you, no friends able to take you in, and no suitable accommodation for Jamie and James. We all know you have to get out of here, which was easy when you only had Jamie but leaving Thomas now without a proper plan in place will not work."*

Carole quickly realises she is in a hopeless predicament at that time and changes her mind.

Carole knew Thomas was regularly using illegal drugs and drinking more than he admitted but whenever she talked to him about his drugs and alcohol abuse, he tried to convince her he was neither a drug addict nor an alcoholic. Sometimes he slurred his words or fall asleep during a conversation, wake up in an aggressive mood and start an argument about something unconnected with the original conversation. Such deviations often confuse Carole, which Thomas used as a premise for continuing an argument and subsequent violence.

Drug Impact On The Family

If you don't get a good result from what you're doing, you might not be doing it wrong, just try doing it differently.

The issues associated with illegal drugs are mostly talked about as a teenage and young adult problem but the problem is also an older adult problem, which might be a parent—mother or father, other family member or friend.

The impact of the problem on one member of the family, can, at best be traumatic, and at worse devastating on the rest of the family, particularly when it escalates to sexual molestation, abuse and sustained physical violence.

The use of illegal drugs within the family, in particular by the parents, creates as well as increases risks, such as the likelihood that the child or children might pick up the habit and develop serious health and drug related problems later.

The deterioration of the physical and psychological quality of life in children and young adults might be linked to the problems associated with the use of illegal drugs. Such problems will ultimately have a profound negative affect on the way the family deal with everyday problems.

Other significant conflicts can develop, brought about by the need for money to buy the drugs. For example, stealing regular sums of money or stealing personal and expensive valuables. Whilst selling the valuables might benefit the drug user financially, stealing money can create a negative impact on the families' finance, which in turn will influence the families' standard of living.

The involvement in illegal drugs might begin at home but exposure to the drugs might begin at school, in sport or as an experiment. Relationships, family included, often suffer, ranging from separation to divorce as the drug problem becomes overwhelming, creating some of the emotional issues associated with bereavement such as, anger, anxiety and fear. It also cerates fear of shame, rejection and isolation. Stress and anxiety sometimes occurs when protective measures are put into practice that will protect those in the family who are vulnerable. These measures might include some form of deprivation, counselling or treatment for addiction.

A Fateful Event

The good thing about being right is not making others feel bad about being wrong.

It is the morning after a night of verbal abuse and violence. Carole manages to hide and disguise some the bruises but struggles to hide the pain before waking Jamie and James. Thomas taunts and ridicules her but she is in too much pain to protest—not that it would make any difference, as she prepares Jamie and James for school. Jamie knows from the raised voices and thuds that came from her parents' room during the night, her Mum is physically and mentally hurting. She takes a long look at Carole before setting off for school and James takes a final look at the television.

Thomas gets up from the dining table, checks that Jamie and James are out of sight, locks the door and engages one of the bolts, and continues taunting Carole. Carole is apprehensive and sits on the settee to avoid being knocked over if she is attacked but he pulls her sideways onto the settee by her hair with such force she winces but does not protest. He rages and intimidates her throwing furniture and ornaments across the room, and scattering cutlery onto the kitchen floor. Thomas is ready to leave the house but before doing so, he gives Carole a warning; "*If this place isn't tidy by the time I get back, you'd better have a fucking good reason.*"

Carole composes herself, finishes her ablutions and prepares for the task in hand. She is frantic with worry, she is in pain from the beating the night before, she is desperately trying to get the house in order but the pain is hindering her progress. It is near the end of the day and the room is a little untidy with several ornaments and furniture still out of place. She is also busy preparing dinner for Jamie and James who are due home shortly, and is anxious that they finish the meal and go upstairs before Thomas arrive home.

Jamie and James arrives home from school, walks into the sitting room before taking off their shoes and coats, and greets Carole in the usual way. "*Hi Mum, Hi Mum, are you all right Mum? Where is Dad? We're hungry.*" The greeting from Jamie on that occasion is not routine or part of their upbringing; it is to *check* if Carole has any more injuries such as a black eye, swollen lips or a bandaged arm.

James runs into the kitchen; "*Hi Mum, are we having burgers today? My friend Jason says he can have burgers all the time. Can we have burgers all the time? Will Dad have burgers as well?*" Carole is aware that a routine is been broken and reminds them, "*You know you should take off your shoes in the house. Do not leave your bags there. Go upstairs and take off your school cloths. Go on, hurry up and eat your dinner before your Dad gets home. James, don't switch on the TV yet,*" but he ignores Carole and turn on the television.

Carole rarely raises her voice to the children but she is angry that James has disobeyed her and in a raised voice reminds him, "*James, I told you not to turn on the TV. Turn it off—now.*"

James is not used to Carole raising her voice at him and is startled. He looks at her for a few seconds, turns and runs up to his room without turning off the television. Carole is worried that James might be afraid of her and calls him back. *"James, James come here. I am sorry I shouted at you. I didn't mean to scare you. I still love you. Go upstairs and take off your school uniform."* She kisses him on the forehead and goes back into the kitchen. James turns away and is on his way back upstairs but remembers why Carole shouted at him and turns off the television.

Carole finishes preparing the meal, brings it to the table and calls out, *"Come on, go and sit down, come on, and hurry up before your Dad gets home."*

Jamie and James prepares to leave the room after dinner but before leaving, Jamie takes another long look at Carole and pushes James towards the hallway door preventing him from switching on the television and goes back upstairs.

About twenty minutes later, Thomas arrives home. He quietly opens the front door, goes into the sitting room, switches on the television and softly calls, *"Carole, Carole"* then in a loud voice, almost screaming, *"Carole, Carole."* The fierceness of his voice startles Carole and she responds, *"Sorry Thomas, I didn't hear you the first time, sorry. How long have you been home? Sorry, I'll listen out for you next time. Your dinner will soon be ready."* He ignores her apologies and explanations, sits at the table and snarls, *"Where the fuck was you? I've been shouting my fucking head off. What are you playing at? Where is my dinner? I'm starving."*

Carole is in a quandary. The tone of his voice is enough to make her think twice about verbally responding, yet, ignoring him would antagonise him more and invoke his wrath. She is anxious that Jamie and James might be listening to Thomas and after the brief pause responds, not knowing Thomas is already sitting down. *"You sit down and I'll bring it. What do you want to drink with it?"* Thomas replies, *"What do you mean sit down? I am sitting down and my dinner should be sitting down with me but it's not. I've been out all day; I come home and can't get a fucking thing to eat."* Thomas gets up before Carole brings his dinner, he goes into the kitchen, grabs her hair as she is picking up the plate but she manages to put it down before he pushes her head against the refrigerator.

Carole thinks it is best not to plea for mersey at that time as it might fuel his determination to hurt her. He presses his nose against hers and venomously snarls, *"You taking the piss or what? Where is my fucking dinner? What the fuck have you been doing all day? It had better be on the table by the time I sit down again."* He pulls her off the fridge and pushes her towards the cooker; she stumbles, catches her hip on the edge of the worktop and collides with the kitchen sink. Carole is hurt but does not complain, instead, reassures Thomas, *"Sorry, sorry Thomas, I was tidying up for you. You go and sit down and I'll bring it now."* Thomas mutters on his way back to the table, *"If you weren't such a lazy cow you'd have it ready for when I get home."* He pauses, looks back and demands, *"Hurry up."*

To call a woman a Cow is a compliment. Cows are useful, gentle, caring and loving.

Although Jamie and James have become accustomed to hearing Thomas raising his voice to Carole, they are particularly disturbed because earlier Carole raised her voice to James. They can hear Thomas's raised voice coming from the dining area and later in the kitchen but cannot hear Carole's' voice. Jamie is worried, she disobeys Carole and goes downstairs. She cautiously goes into the sitting room and looks at Thomas who is sitting at the table. James follows Jamie into the sitting room, looks at the television, thinks it is an opportunity to watch the television, and asks, *"Can I watch the TV?"* James is unsure if he can watch the television because no one answers him. James knows he should be upstairs but as Jamie is downstairs, he feels it is sufficient for him to watch the television.

While pondering his next move to get permission, James greets Thomas with, *"Hi Dad didn't hear you come home. Have you had your dinner?"*

Jamie acknowledges Thomas is in the house but does not speak with him; instead, she goes into the kitchen where Carole is sobbing quietly. Carole is angry that Jamie sees her crying and retorts, *"I told you two to stay upstairs and let your Dad have his dinner in peace. Go on; now, take James with you and go back upstairs—now."* Carole turns her head and wipes the tears from her face.

Thomas answers James, *"Hi Tiger, no. I am still waiting for that shit your mother is making. Was your dinner better than mine will be? Your stupid mother is always trying to stop you and me from having a chat. Come here, did you smack anyone in the mouth today?"* James quickly responds, *"No, I don't smack my best friends 'cause I like them. Jason is my bestist friend. His mum said I could go to his house anytime. Can Jason come to our house anytime?"* Thomas ignores James' question. As Jamie walks back into the sitting room, Thomas asks, *"What about you Jamie, have you made any fairy cakes today? Did you fart about on that stage contraption? I hope you get a proper job when you bloody grow up, not like your mother, (in aloud voice) the stupid lazy cow."*

Jamie does not reply. She is worried because she thinks something is wrong with Carole and is determined to remain downstairs as long as possible, so she disobeys Carole. James knows it is not a good time to ask if he can watch the television since Carole has repeated her instructions to go back upstairs, so he points at the television as if pointing will switch it on. Jamie avoids antagonising Thomas by not answering his questions or commenting on his suggestion, instead, pretends she is talking to Carole. *"Mum, can I have some—"* Carole interrupts, *"Don't bother me now; I'm giving your Dad his dinner. Now please go back upstairs—both of you—'till later."*

Thomas has no idea what Jamie is asking for but sarcastically intervenes; *"Don't stop her now, your Mum cant do two things at once so do what she says before she forgets my dinner—that's if she's made it."*

James thinks he should try again to watch the television but this time he includes Jamie in his quest and asks, *"Dad, can we watch the TV?"* Carole overhears James asking if he can watch the television and angrily repeats, *"Jamie, James, get upstairs, I won't tell you again."* Jamie and James leave the room looking somewhat dejected and goes back upstairs.

Children Trapped In Domestic Violence

It is not always the good soil that produces the good crops; it's the good care the crops receive.

In ninety percent of domestic incidents, at least one child is present, or several children might be in an adjoining room. The child or children might be sent to another room to be out of the way or might have escaped to another room fearing escalation of the abuse. The correlation between physical abuse against a child or children, and domestic violence is inseparable and unfortunately prevalent. It is also understood that at least seventy percent of children living in refuges were abused by the male parent.

Annually, around 275 million children worldwide suffer the consequences of a turbulent home life instigated by domestic abuse. The abuse against children might be physical, psychological, neglect, exploitation or sexual. The wrong doers might include a parent, parents; close family members, close associates of the family and in many reported instances, strangers, which might be referred to as sex offenders. Those children who survive domestic abuse often suffer long-term psychological damage, which decreases their ability to learn—academically, socialise and lead normal lives.

Children growing up in an abusive or violent environment are more likely to be victims of abuse within that environment or otherwise, compared to children who have grown up in a non-abusive or violent environment. However, there is no certainty that children from a violent background will naturally become victims of abuse, or become abusers, or that children from a non-abusive or non-violent background will not become abusers.

The behavioural and psychological consequences for children growing up with domestic abuse and relentless violence can be irrevocably damaging. For example, children who are exposed to domestic violence often suffer various symptoms of stress disorder, such as anxiety, depression, bed-wetting or nightmares, and are at greater risk of suffering from a variety of allergies. Such children are more likely to consider or attempt suicide, and or become alcoholics or drug addicts at an early age.

The effects of violence or violent behaviour tends to stay with children long after leaving the original source of the abuse, which is usually their first home, and, unless appropriate help and support is forthcoming at the early stages of the unacceptable behaviour pattern, the effects might be passed to future generations. Boys who are exposed to domestic violence are twice as likely to become abusive men. Furthermore, girls who witness domestic abuse against their mother are more likely to accept abuse and violence in a relationship than girls who come from non-violent homes.

A mother's first instinct is to protect her young from harm or danger. Mothers who suffer abuse in domestic situations, often provide protection for the children that are exposed to the violence despite being unable to protect themselves. However, a high percentage of women and children remain trapped and unprotected in abusive and violent situations, because they might not have the financial resources to obtain protection through the legal system or because of the psychological or financial control by the abuser. Without the capacity to access meaningful support and protection, the abuse is likely to continue

Thomas is sitting at the table and is tapping the place mat rhythmically with his right-hand fingers whilst staring menacingly at the kitchen door. Carole takes the meal to Thomas, but remembers she has not asked him if he wants his usual drink. Thomas does not have a usual drink, but Carole is playing safe by remembering the last one she gave him, which in fact, might not be the last one he had. He stares at the food, turns the plate full circle, looks across the room and clenches his fist.

James is agitated; he goes into Jamies' room and sits on her bed without speaking.

Jamie is perplexed, worried about her Mum, angry with her Dad and has little time for James and snarls, *"What are you doing in my room? You should be in your own room, get out, go on, get out."* James ignores her and remarks, *"Our Mum isn't stupid, is she? She makes our breakfast and gets our dinner ready for when we come home. What is a lazy cow? Can we have one? Our Mum sometimes cries like a baby but she's not stupid, is she?"* Jamie does not answer his questions because her thoughts are elsewhere but replies, *"Dad and Mum are always shouting but Dad does most of the shouting. Mum always seems to upset Dad, and then he thumps her. She doesn't play with us like she used to because she is always hurting."* James is about to say something but Jamie stops him. *"Shurrup and leave me alone. I am sick of all the shouting and Mum crying. I'm going downstairs to see my Mum."*

James remembers what happened the last time he disobeyed Carole and reminds Jamie, *"We have to stay up here until Mum says is OK to go down. I don't want Mum shouting at me again. Dad thinks you are a Fairy and me a Tiger. I am a Tiger, but I am not going eat anyone. I'll come home for Mum to give me my breakfast and make my dinner."* Jamie is becoming more anxious after seeing Carole crying and is impatient with James. She ponders for a while then stands up, looks through the window, paces around her room, throws her teddy at the window and begins to cry. She is whimpering and snarls at James, *"I said shurrup, shurrup I don't want to talk bout it. I want to go downstairs to my Mum"* and falls face down onto her bed sobbing and kicking. James leaves the room but quickly returns and begins to cry.

Carole is afraid to approach the table in case Thomas lash out or throw the food at her, so, from the safety of the kitchen she asks, *"Do you want a beer with your dinner Thomas?"* After looking at each item of food on the plate, he mutters, *"Yes, it's probably better than this fucking shit you dish up."* Carole ignores the remark and reassures him, *"I'm bringing it now."*

Jamie is struggling mentally to find the answer to who starts the shouting, when it will stop and what is happening to Carole. She turns and stares at James without speaking. James slowly goes to Jamie and gives her a hug. She hugs James and together they weep uncontrollably. James asks, *"When will Dad stop shouting at our Mum?"* In her frustration, Jamie replies, *"I don't know. I don't know don't ask me. You keep asking me all these questions."* With anger in her voice, she grits her teeth, *"Will you shurrup."*

Carole opens the can of beer but her hand is shaking and she spills some as she pours it into the glass. The beer is just below the full mark on the glass. Carole nervously picks up the glass; her hand is shaking and considers pouring the beer into a smaller glass but discounts that thought, because she knows Thomas will recognise it is not his beer glass. Although Thomas do not have meals with the children, he insists Carole remain, either in the sitting room or in the kitchen, just in case he want something or something else. However, Carole decides she will give him his beer as it is and go upstairs to be with Jamie and James.

James asks, *"Is our Mum lazy? She is always doing things when we come home and she tells us things so she is not stupid or lazy. Our teacher tells us things but she doesn't make our breakfast or dinner."* *"Shurrup"* Jamie snaps, *"Teachers aren't supposed to get us our breakfast or dinner."*

Thumping the table aggressively, Thomas remarks, *"About fucking time. You, come here. What-is-this-shit?"* Carole is cautiously on her way to the table with Thomas' beer but hurries when she hears the question. She is about to put the beer on the table but with her hand shaking she spills some onto the table. The beer is now noticeably below the full mark and Carole is noticeably worried. It doesn't take long for Thomas to notice the short measure. He stands up, kicks the chair behind him, picks up the knife and points it at Carole. *"You dozy cow. You are going nowhere. I want a full glass of beer not half a glass. I bought a full can and I want a full can. I don't work my arse off for you to give me this fucking shit and half a glass of beer."* He grabs her hair, yanks her head back as he picks up the beer. Carole sees him picking up the beer and holds onto the back of a chair to keep her balance. She pleads with him not to hurt her and begins to cry.

Jamie and James moves into his room because it is not directly over the dining room, but are worried because they cannot hear Thomas or Carole. Jamie thinks it is better to hear them shouting, and moves back into her room. Jamie is more anxious and remarks, *"I can hear Dad but I can't hear Mum. Why is Mum not talking?"* James is quick to remind Jamie, *"We have to stay upstairs until Mum say it is OK to go downstairs."* Jamie replies, *"I know, but what if Mum wants to talk to us or shows us something? She might want us to get something for her or wash-up after Dad finishes his dinner so that she can have a rest and—."* James interrupts, *"Or Dad might let us watch the TV."*

Carole is desperate and pleads with Thomas, *"Please, please Thomas, please don't hurt me any more. The children are upstairs and might come down to watch the TV. Tell me what you want and I'll get it for you. Sorry I spilled your beer; I won't spill any more again. Don't mark my face for the children to see. Please Thomas, don't hurt me, I think I missed my period. I'm sorry."* Thomas rants: *"You'll be fucking sorry. Take this rubbish out to my sight and get me some proper food. What do you do with all the fucking money I give you? Are you taking the piss?"* Thomas lets go of Carole's hair but she cannot move because he is standing on her foot. He puts the glass back on the table, picks up the plate and empties the food over her head. The food runs down her face temporally blinding her but she is able to back away and wipes the food from her head and face as she does so. Thomas picks up the glass of beer again, throws the beer forcefully into her face and says, *"You stupid lazy cow, you'll pay for this once and for all."* The force of the liquid on her face makes her gasp for breath.

Thomas throws the empty glass onto the table, lashes out and strikes Carole with the back of his left hand just

111

above her temple. She is dazed from the force of the blow; she staggers backwards, raises her left hand to protect her head and continues wiping the food from her face with her right hand. Carole is still trying to maintain her balance while staggering backwards.

Carole's vision is blurred but she is able to see Thomas's foot as he kicks out at her. He misses because she is just out of range. She pleads with him again. *"No, no, please don't, no, tell me what you want, tell me and I'll get it. Don't let Jamie and James see me like this. Don't kick me just in case I'm preg—"* She pauses then continues, *"I, I can't see properly and my head feels funny. Please, let me sit down for a minute, please,"* but her pleading appears to fuel his aggression. Thomas ignores her and in a particularly aggressive tone responds, *"I'll tell you what I don't bloody want, and that's a fucking lazy cow."*

Carole stumbles into the sitting room and falls backwards onto the settee but instinctively gets up and continues pleading with Thomas not to hit her but he ignores her. His expression changes as he lashes out with a clenched fist striking her on the other side of the head. The ferocity of the blow makes Carole groan; she becomes disorientated after loosing her vision and her balance.

Jamie and James move back into his room and turns on the radio. The sound coming from downstairs is muffled by the radios' volume but Jamie is worried again because she cannot hear Carole and tells James, *"Turn off the radio, I can't hear Mum."* James is confused and responds, *"But you said you don't want to hear Mum and Dad."* Jamie replies, *"I don't but I want to hear if Mum calls and want me to do something."* James is still confused and tearfully tells Jamie, *"I want to go back to your room. I'm scared."* Jamie agrees, *"Yeah, come we can listen to my radio."* James looks at Jamie in total confusion and remarks, *"But if you turn it on we wont be able to hear Mum if—"* Jamie interrupts, *"Shruup, you don't know anything."*

The force of the blow sends Carole tottering back into the dining area, she collides with the corner of the dining table and slowly falls face down onto the floor. Carole convulses for a few minutes, she is motionless and does not speak. Thomas hurries across the room to Carole and as she lies on the floor he demands, *"Get up you lazy cow, I said get up,"* and kicks her twice on the buttocks but she is still motionless and does not attempt to get up. He jabs her in the side and to the head, repeating after each jab, *"Get up, get up, fucking get up, get up, I said get up."* He stops jabbing but Carole is still lying motionless. He steps back and stares at Carole's motionless body but makes no attempt to pick her up and casually walks away muttering, *"The fucking lazy cow. I'll sort her out when she gets up."* He goes back to Carole and gestures *"Don't think you can lie there all day doing fuckall. Get up or I'll give it to you—if that's what you want—is it? Well, is it?"* Carole urinates uncontrollably but Thomas ignores her condition and comments, *"You're not only a lazy cow but now you're being a dirty cow lying in your own piss and shit."*

James is restless, he opens Jamie's bedroom door and stands for a few seconds before leaving the room. He hurries back to Jamie and reports, *"I can't hear Mum or Dad shouting or talking."*

Jamie stands outside her room and listens but does not hear Thomas or Carole. She goes back into the room, paces back and forth and defiantly declares, *"I'm going downstairs to my Mum, you coming?"* James is worried that he might be disobeying his Mum and reminds Jamie again they have to remain upstairs until she says it is all right to go downstairs.

Jamie is determine to go downstairs and justifies her decision by reminding James, *"My Mum didn't shout at me, it was you she shouted at, so I can go down. You can stay up here if you want to."* James have no desire to disobey his Mum but he feels he must to go downstairs and see her, so he suggests, *"I'm coming with you but you go into the room first and ask Dad if I can watch the TV."* Jamie agrees, *"All right, but I'm going down now. Are you coming?"*

Jamie and James go downstairs together holding hands but James remains in the hallway. Jamie is apprehensive as she enters the sitting room first. She stares at Thomas but from where she is standing, she can only see the soles of Carole's feet. Jamie steps back, pulls James into the room, stands next to the settee holding hands and looks at Thomas who is standing a few feet from the dining table. James looks around the sitting room, then the dining area and sees Carole lying on the floor almost under the dining table.

Thomas looks at Jamie and James somewhat sternly, and reminds them of what Carole said earlier about staying upstairs. *"Your Mum told both of you to stay upstairs, didn't she? I told you to do what your Mother says. Don't bother her now, she's having a little lie down after all that hard work fetching my dinner."* Jamie ignores Thomas and hurries over to Carole, kneels next to her, holds her hand and shakes her shoulder without speaking, while James remains standing next to the settee.

Thomas walks around in circles and gesticulates at the food and beer on the floor. *"Look at this mess. It is her fault. It's your Mums fault."* He kicks some of the food across the floor and scrapes his foot across the spilled beer. The food, beer and urine create a pungent odour, prompting Thomas to comment, *"It stinks in here. It is her fault. It's your Mums fault."*

Jamie leans over and speaks to Carole *as* she gently moves Carole's hair to one side but let go when she sees the food on her face. *"Muum, why are you sleeping on the floor? Muum, Muum wake up."* Jamie continues, *"Wake up Muum. Muum, you have food in your hair and on your face. Wake up please. Muum, I want you to wake up now."* Jamie stops talking, sits on her heels and, as if she is scanning Carole's body, looks at her from head to heel several times. She pauses for a few seconds, looks up at Thomas and asks, *"Dad, why is Mum lying on the floor? Why is her hair red in places? Does Mum want to go to the toilet?"* James sets off to join Jamie but he feels intimidated by the menacing stare from Thomas and goes back into the sitting room.

Thomas pretends to be distracted by James and ignores Jamie. She stands up and steps back, looks at Thomas then at Carole and without speaking, walks towards James who is staring nervously at Thomas, holds James's hand, leaves the room and goes back upstairs side by side and in silence. Jamie goes to her room and James runs into his room but quickly runs back to Jamie's room. Jamie stares out of the window; James stares at her and asks, *"Why is Mum lying down?* Jamie does not reply but leaves the room, stands at the top of the stairs and stares at the front door.

The windows downstairs, including the kitchen window are closed, and the odour from the food, beer and urine has drifted upstairs. James is concerned and asks, *"What is that funny smell? Did Mum want to go to the toilet?"* Jamie returns to her room in silence and sits on the bed.

Thomas goes over to Carole again, kicks her leg and in a calmer voice demands, *"Get up you. Stop messing about. Now get up. Jamie and James came to see you but they've gone back upstairs so you can get up and stop fucking pretending."* He looks at Carole's motionless body, bends over her, moves her head from side to side and steps back. He recognises Carole is seriously hurt but does nothing to help her. He places one hand over his mouth and murmurs, *"Oh fuh fuck sakes, what have I done? Jeeesus krice what have I done?"* He picks up the plate and beer glass, washes them, returns to the dining area and cleans the food off the table and the floor. He begins cleaning the food off Carole's face and cloths but stops and tidies the room instead.

Thomas goes back to Carole after tidying the room; he kneels beside her and cleans the remainder of food from her face and blood from her ear. He tries cleaning the blood from her hair but stops, walks away, stares at the ceiling and mutters, *"I think I'd better leave her alone. Maybe I shouldn't touch her after the accident. She might get up later. She is always walking into things and banging her self—proper accident-prone. I had better tell Jamie not to touch her in case she bangs her head on the table when she gets up. I wonder if I should get her a clean pair of knickers, I'll see if there's one in the washing machine. Krice, what have I done, it's her fault, it's her fucking fault, it's her fucking fault."*

After a few minutes, Thomas returns, strokes her face, straightens her hair but does not clean it and covers her ears. He goes back into the kitchen and puts the clean dishes in the cupboard, checks the washing machine and mops the kitchen floor. He goes back to Carole and makes sure her cloths are tidy without altering her physical position and steps back without speaking. He puts on his coat, stands as if to attention awaiting the command to salute and in a non-aggressive voice speaks to Carole, *"I've tidied up and put the dishes away. The washing machine is working and the windows are closed."* However, as if to remind Carole there is no change to his expectations he continues, *"I'm going out and you had better be up when I get back."*

Thomas walks in a military slow march fashion into the sitting room, pauses, looks back at Carole, glances around the room and continues to the front door. He stands in the Hallway for a few seconds, looks upstairs but goes back into the sitting room and sits on the settee for a few minutes with his hands under his chin. He stands up, looks at Carole and mutters, *"Pretending, that's all she does, fucking pretend. Pretends she can cook, pretends she can keep the house clean, pretends she loves me, pretends she loves the kids, pretends she have no friends. I'll kick her arse when I get back."* He goes back into the Hallway and looks up the stairs, puts one foot on the first step but steps back and turns to the front door. He quietly opens the door but slams it shut as he leaves the house.

Reactions

Strength is not always measured by what or how much is carried but by how it's endured.

Jamie hears the door slams; she wait's a few moments before looking through her bedroom window but cannot see Thomas. James tentatively looks down the stairs and into the Hallway but cannot see or hear anyone. Defiantly, Jamie says, *"I'm going down to see my Mum. I think Dad's gone out."* James agrees. *"Me too, wait for me. If Mum is still lying down you can't pick her up 'cause you're a Fairy but I can pick her up 'cause I'm a Tiger."* Jamie looks at James, smirks and shakes her head.

Together they quickly run to where Carole is lying motionless. James is unperturbed at that time; he goes back into the sitting room and switches on the television. Jamie takes Carole's hand, pulls it three times and sobs with each pull. *"Mum, wake up, Mum wake up, Mum wake up please."*

James switches off the television; he strolls into the dining area and asks Jamie, *"Why is Mum still lying there? Do you want me to pick her up? Did my Dad not like his dinner?"*

Jamie does not answer so James goes back into the sitting room and switches on the television.

Jamie is frantic and runs to James, then to the front door. She looks at the closed door but does not open it; instead, she runs upstairs but changes her mind after the first five steps and runs back into the sitting room. She calls out; *"Dad, Dad. Where is Dad?"*

James is watching the television but is unsure what to do and switches it off and on.

Jamie looks around the sitting room for a few seconds, runs into the kitchen, checks the window and door are closed, and goes back to Carole. She kneels next to Carole, has a closer look at her face and weeps uncontrollably.

James sees Jamie crying and hurries over to her. They hold onto each other whilst kneeling. James calls out, *"I want my Mum to get up. Why don't you make Mum get up? If Dad was here he would pick her up."*

Jamie replies, *"I'll go and look for Dad and tell him Mum is still lying on the floor, 'cause he told Mum to get up for when he gets back."*

Jamie and James let go each other and stands up. James goes back into the sitting room and Jamie goes outside to look for Thomas without telling James but there is no one outside. James calls Jamie but she does not answer. He panics, runs upstairs and comes back down, stomping heavily on the stairs. He is crying and calls, *"Jamie, Jamie, Jamie. I want my Mum. Jamie. Where is Dad?"* He pauses as he enters the sitting room and as loud as he could, calls out for Jamie.

Jamie comes back into the house through the kitchen and flops heavily on the settee. *"I can't see Dad or any of his friends. I want to tell Dad Mum is still lying down."* James replies, *"He might come back later. Is Samantha coming to see*

Mum?" Jamie pauses then replies, *"I don't know but if she is coming, she will have to leave before Dad comes home."*

James asks, *"Will Gloria and Patricia come too? I think they will come because they are Mum's best friends."*

Jamie is impatient with James and sharply replies, *"You're asking me too many questions. I don't know where Gloria or Patricia lives or how to telephone them. I'm going to ask Mum to wake up." Jamie* remains on the settee with her head in her hands rocking back and forth.

The odour in the house is becoming more pungent.

James runs to the front door and shouts, *"Fucking, fucking, fucking, fuckup."* Jamie is crying and screaming as she rushes to James. She lashes out in anger but not to connect, and in a screeching tone tells James, *"Don't say that word. Do not say that word. Stop it. Stop it. Don't say that word."* James is taken aback by Jamie's outburst and begins crying. *"Is that a bad word? I'll not say it again. Sorry, I'll not say it again. I hear my Dad say it but I'll not say it again."* He runs to Jamie, they hug each other and weeps openly.

James goes over to Carole; he moves her head to one side and is excited when he sees the colour of her lips. He calls out to Jamie, *"Look, Jamie look, Mums' put on some lipstick, a blue one. Come and look."* Jamie wipes the tears from her eyes and off her cheeks, and hurries over to Carole. *"That's not lip stick."* James is somewhat despondent with his observation and asks, *"What is it. What is it?"* Jamie knows it is not lipstick but she takes a closer look and replies, *"I don't know but it's not lip stick. I've never seen Mum with that colour lipstick and I don't see it on the floor."*

Jamie goes to the front door; ponders for a few seconds and opens the door. James is nervous and asks, *"Can you see Dad or any of Dad's friends?"* Jamie replies, *"No"* closes the door and slowly goes back into the sitting room. She looks around and, trembling uncontrollably, urinates as she walks back towards the dining area. James sees Jamie trembling and urinating, and is unsure how to react but in a moment of thoughtfulness he asks, *"Do you think Mum wants to go to the toilet? I want to go to the toilet as well but I don't want to go in case Mum wants to go first when she gets up.* Jamie is embarrassed and mutters, *"I don't know. I'm going to call the Ambulance but I don't know what to say."* James is suddenly excited that the Ambulance will be coming to the house. *"Yeah, the Ambulance, will it have the siren going nee nah nee nah nee nah and lights flashing? Yeah, I want to see that."*

Jamie is frustrated with James and snaps, *"Shurrup. Shurrup. Where's Dad?"* and goes to the telephone but before picking it up, she goes back to see if Carole is moving. Carole is not moving so she hurries back to the telephone, picks it up and taps 999 but replaces the receiver before the operator answers.

James picks up the telephone but is unsure what to do. *"Which number do I press? Is it this one or that one? Will it keep ringing if I keep pressing the numbers?"* He is frustrated and slams the receiver. Jamie is crying profusely and goes back to Carole.

"Mum, what do I tell the Ambulance? I don't know what to tell them. Muuum, will you get up, please? I don't know where Dad is and I don't know where Samantha is. Mum, are Gloria and Patricia coming to see you? Muum, Muum, Muum." Jamie strolls back to James, still crying, snatches the telephone and taps 999. The operator answers, *"Police, Fire or Ambulance?"* Jamie doesn't respond but stares at James. The operator repeats in a stern voice, *"Police, Fire or Ambulance. I know you are there so stop wasting our time. Which service would you like? Is this is an emergency?"* Jamie is momentarily frightened and, unable to speak, replaces the

receiver and together they slowly goes back to Carole, leans over and checks again to see if she is moving.

James steps back from the table; he runs to the front door and attempts to open it but turns away and runs upstairs. He goes from room to room calling, *"Dad, Dad are you in here? Dad, come and pick up Mum, she is still lying down."* He is terrified, screams, hurries down stairs, runs into the kitchen screaming, and goes to the telephone followed by Jamie. He attempts to pick it up but steps back and begins to tremble. Jamie picks it up again, begins sobbing, and taps 999.

The operator answers, *"Police, Fire or Ambulance?"* Jamie does not respond immediately but looks at James and begins sobbing. Her voice is barely audible as she speaks to the operator. *"Ca ca can you send the Ambulance please? Ca ca can it come now?"* James is anxious and impatient, and asks, *"Is the Ambulance coming now? I can't hear it. I can't see the lights. Can I let them in when it comes, can I?"*

The operator recognises it is a child's voice but is unaware of the seriousness of the call and responds, *"Listen, this is an emergency number and you must not use it unless there is an emergency. You can get into trouble with the Police or get your parents into trouble. Who are you? Where are you?"* Jamie sobs as she speaks. *"My name is Jamie and James is my brother."* The operator asks, *"What is your other name?"* Jamie stutters, *"Mine is Jojoyce and my brother is Totoby."* The operator explains; *"I don't mean your middle name. What is your parents' last name?"* Jamie is confused; she looks at James, and replaces the receiver. *"I don't know what Mum and Dads' last name is. I don't know what to tell the Ambulance."*

Jamie picks up the receiver again and taps 999. The operator answers *"Police, Fire or Ambulance?"* Jamie responds quicker. *"Please, can you send the Ambulance?"* The operator recognises Jamie's' voice. *"Are you the little girl who called a moment ago? Where do you live?"* Jamie answers, *"We live at number 13 Hardman Drive."* The operator is not familiar with Jamie or James but immediately recognises the address and nonchalantly replies. *"Oh yes, we know that address. What is it this time sweetheart?"*

Jamie does not answer but looks at James. James begins sobbing loudly and Jamie takes a long look at Carole. The operator hears James sobbing and in a calmer voice asks, *"Is someone there feeling poorly? Don't be afraid sweetheart; you can talk to me because I want to help you and your brother or anyone else."* The operator pauses then asks, *"Why do you want the Ambulance to come to your house?"* Jamie replies, *"I don't know where my Dad is. I don't know what time Samantha or Gloria or Patricia is coming to see Mum and all the windows are closed."*

The operator senses the panic in Jamie's voice, the confusion in her response and tries not to exacerbate the situation. *"Jamie, where is your Mum and Dad?"* Jamie answers, *"I don't know where Dad is."*

The operator asks, *"Can I speak to your Mum?"* Jamie stares at the telephone after hearing the question, then looks at Carole and in a moment of confusion, puts down the receiver and hurries over to Carole. *"Muum, Muum, get up. The woman on the telephone wants to talk to you."* She goes back to the telephone but it rings before she reaches it. They both panic and scream at the unexpected ringing and Jamie in thrown into utter confusion.

The telephone continues ringing as she runs back to Carole. *"Mum, the phone is ringing; the woman wants to talk to you."* James hit the telephone in a bid to stop it ringing but it continues ringing. He hits it again and this time it stops but the sudden silence creates further confusion. They look at each other before Jamie suddenly remembers why she went over to Carole and goes to pick up the telephone but stares at it in bewilderment. She picks it up and without tapping 999, speaks. *"My Dad is not here yet and Samantha is not here" but* there is no response only the dial tone. She looks at the telephone, replaces the receiver and picks it up again but before tapping 999 she hears a voice, *"Hello, is that you Jamie? It's ok; please don't put down the phone on me. I want to help. Can you hear me Jamie?"* Jamie answers, *"Yes, but Dad is not here."*

The operator begins a conversation. *"OK. I know your name is Jamie and your brother is James. Can you tell me what your Dad's name is?"*

Jamie and James have never called Thomas or Carole by their first name, so she is unsure how to answer the question and replies, *"My Dad is Dad but he's not here and my Mum is Mum."* James is hysterical, shouts, *"Is the Ambulance coming now?"* and runs to the front door. The operator speaks to Jamie. *"Tell James the Ambulance in on its way,"* but Jamie does not pass on the message. The operator asks again, *"Can I please speak to your Mum now Jamie?"*

A good friend is never lost, just absent.

There is a knock at the front door. James runs to the door, he sees the reflection of the Ambulance and hurries back to Jamie. He does not speak, instead he points to the door. Jamie slowly lowers the receiver, and lets it go as the operator is speaking. She pulls James close to her and holding hands, walks slowly to the front door. There is another knock just as they reach the door.

Jamie opens the door and looks at the Paramedics first, and then she looks at the ambulance and at the Paramedics again. The Paramedics step back and cover their mouths for a moment because the stench inside the house is particularly pungent. A Paramedic asks, *"Are you Jamie and James?"* Neither of them answers but stares at the Ambulance. The Paramedic asks, *"Is it your Mum or your Dad we come to see?"* Neither of them answers. The Paramedic asks, *"Can we come in to see who need our help?"* Neither of them answers. The Paramedic asks, *"Can you tell us why we are here?"* Jamie is trembling as she rubs her ankles together. Unable to contain her emotions, she takes a step back and exclaims, ***"My Mummy won't wake up."***

Samantha arrives a few minutes after the Ambulance.

Jamie and James lead the Paramedics through the sitting room and into the dining area without speaking. They stand side by side still holding each other's hand and watches as the Paramedics examine Carole.

The dining table is lifted to one side to allow the Paramedics to cover Carole with a sheet.

Jamie and James watches and whimpers as Carole is lifted onto the stretcher, and follows as she is carried to the Ambulance.

Side by side they stand at the door as Carole is lifted into the Ambulance.

The Ambulance doors closes slowly allowing Jamie and James a longer look at the covered shape of Carole.

The Ambulance drives away slowly without its siren sounding or its lights flashing.

James looks at Jamie with tears in his eyes and asks, *"Will Mum wake up?"*

Jamie watches the Ambulance until it drives out of sight; she turns to James with tears running down her cheeks and tells him, *"Shurrup."*

Samantha asks, *"Jamie, where is your Dad?"*

Jamie takes James to the dining area, stands for a few minutes then kneels under the table near the soiled section of the floor where Carole fell.

Samantha asks again, "Jamie, do you know where your dad is?"

Jamie answers, ***"My Mummy won't wake up."***

About The Author

Alvis Younge, known to his friends as Ollie, was born in beautiful Barbados and lived in England after serving in the British Army from 1962 to 1968. He has travelled extensively, visiting countries in Europe and Africa as well as America and Canada. He enjoyed a wonderful upbringing, which included a fantastic and unspoiled relationship with his Grandmother.

Alvis begun his working life as a Motor Engineer, referred to in the early years as a Motor Mechanic. During the ascension to his vast and varied life experience, he attained various professional roles; however, from an early age he felt the need to divert from "things mechanical" and pursue the need to help and support people. His religious upbringing was pivotal to the understanding of the spiritual, emotional and psychological needs of those at risk of enduring prolong suffering.

His adult life was decorated with the usual setbacks and disappointments associated with "well that's life," and in 1998, took the decision to dedicate more of his time to supporting victims of crime, helping the bereaved through counselling to understand and work through the various emotional issues associated with death, and those trying to cope following the onset of domestic disruptions. He expanded his experience by working with specific charities, supporting the sick, the young and other adults in the community.

Alvis has written his early years' autobiography, chronicling the first eighteen years of his life, which he presented to his daughter. He has also written several unpublished short stories and enjoys listening to fruitful arguments.

Alvis retains his close association with nature and all things natural by growing as much of his fresh essentials as possible. Despite the various accounts by some academics on climate change, Alvis firmly believe earthlings did not cause climate change, and that we cannot control or stop climate change but should work to manage the changes and challenges presented as the climate changes.

9 781467 889247